CATA...
AT BLACK... ...INN

CATASTROPHE
AT BLACK PONY INN

Christine
Pullein-Thompson

RAVETTE BOOKS

This edition published by Ravette Books Limited 1989

Phototypeset by Input Typesetting Ltd, London
Printed and bound in Great Britain
for Ravette Books Limited,
3 Glenside Estate, Star Road,
Partridge Green, Horsham,
West Sussex RH13 8RA
by Cox & Wyman Ltd,
Reading

ISBN 1 85304 230 7

One
"They're very rich"

The summer was almost over. The winter's hay for the horses had been delivered. The garden chairs put away. School was about to start again. And we had only three elderly guests at Black Pony Inn. That was until Mummy dropped the bombshell, or rather Mum, because recently, for various reasons, we had stopped calling her Mummy. Smiling at us now, she said, "We've got a whole family coming to Black Pony Inn next week. Isn't that fantastic? They're not old either, so they'll sharpen us up a bit."

I didn't want to be sharpened up. I wanted life to go on the same for ever. Colonel Hunter had been with us for years. The other two guests were sisters, and always had what you needed suddenly like sticking plaster, and needles and thread for plaiting manes. They were more like relations than paying guests.

Now Lisa, who is younger than me and more down to earth asked, "Will there be children and if so, how many?"

"A boy and a girl," replied Mum still smiling.

Ben my younger brother, looked at me and said, "There go our rooms again Harriet."

At the same moment James, who was seventeen said, "I don't think it matters what they're like, if they bring in some money."

"I agree," said Dad. "It's money we need and they're bringing horses and dogs too. If they stay long enough we'll be able to build a swimming pool."

"And think how nice that will be," Mum said patting me on the shoulder. "You can swim every morning then Harriet. You and Ben can train for the pony club tetrathlon too, can't you?"

"And their horses? What are they like?" I asked, and now I was unable to keep the excitement out of my voice.

"Show horses is how they described them," replied Mum. "The family are called Abbott by the way – Grace and Pat Abbott and their children are Justin and Tracey. They are waiting to move into a house they've bought. They're very rich. This was the only place they could find, which would take their horses and dogs as well. I'm sure you will like them."

Dad must have met them too, for now he added, "They are very positive. They showed us snapshots and everything they have looks wonderful – dogs, horses, cars, well everything."

"And their children?" asked Lisa.

"Very neat," Dad said.

6

I looked at our parents. Dad has a round face with dark hair which curls when it's wet. Mum has nut brown hair and brown eyes. Dad is bulky, a bit like a dark haired teddy bear, while Mum is more elfin. Now they looked happy which made me think of the bills in red dropping through the letter box every morning. Three paying guests were hardly enough to keep Black Pony Inn going, so they had reason to smile.

As Ben suspected, he and I had to move out of our rooms, so we spent that afternoon which was Saturday, moving our belongings into the attic bedrooms where Lisa usually reigned in solitary splendour. James didn't have to move. he has the smallest room in the house and it's always in chaos.

"It's going to be an invasion isn't it?" asked Ben pushing a lock of fair hair out of his eyes. "And I bet we never get the swimming pool."

"They'll hate James. They won't like him spilling coffee and forgetting things. You know how cross Colonel Hunter gets, and he isn't particularly neat," I said,

We dragged our bedclothes up the attic stairs and made our beds. "Perhaps they'll give us tips if we carry their suitcases," suggested Ben straightening his duvet.

"Tipping's out of date," I said.

"Not among the rich," argued Ben.

Later we went outside to check our horses They were still living out. Liver chestnut

7

Prince and grey Lorraine were gnawing at each other's manes. Ben's dark, brown, Welsh cob Solitaire was grazing alongside piebald Jigsaw whom we sometimes drove in a governess cart. Our first pony, black Limpet cantered across the front paddock to greet us. They were not just our ponies, they were our friends.

"It's been such a fantastic summer," I said.

"They may be nice, Tracey may be quite old, we don't know their ages yet," said Lisa joining us.

"James may fall in love with her," suggested Ben.

"Or you," I added laughing.

"No way," retorted Ben throwing grass at me.

We had tea in the kitchen, while Mum waited on the guests in the sitting room with a new spring in her stride. We ate lots of lardy-cake and home-made flapjacks.

"You look so gloomy. They're a lovely family, you'll like them. And think of the dogs, you know you've always wanted dogs. Well, now you'll have them," Mum said washing up cups and saucers.

"How long will they be here?" Ben asked eating his fifth flapjack.

"Between six and twelve weeks, they're not sure yet," Mum said.

"But that means they might be here at Christmas," I cried. Won't I have my room back by Christmas Eve?"

"Yes, of course, long before that I expect," Mum replied, but she didn't sound certain.

"Think of the dogs," said Ben later mimicking Mum and laughing, while we sat staring at a television programme without really seeing it.

"I hope the dogs are small and sweet," said Lisa counting her pencils. "Dad says that Justin and Tracey won't be going to our school. They're going to St Peter's. They are too posh for the local school," she continued scornfully.

"We mustn't hate them before they're even here," James said.

It was dark outside now. We were sitting in the room, which years and years ago was the servants' hall. It looks out towards the stables and is next to the kitchen, which still has an old pump in it, a bread oven and a huge dresser running the entire length of one wall. Often while we are in the old servants' hall, which is now called the playroom, we imagine servants sitting there – cook, butler, kitchen maid and all the upstairs servants as well. They sit around the large table where we do our homework, eating; the butler at the top is lording it over the others, while a tiny kitchen maid waits on them. For years ago Black Pony Inn was quite an important house. It was called The Manor, then. Newly prosperous Mr Black had built it for his wife and five children. When Mum and Dad turned it into a guest house they called it Black Pony Inn because we already had Limpet. But it's not the sort of inn which sells intoxicating liquor or dinner at pounds and pounds a head. It's just a guest house really where people can stay as long as they like, for a reasonable amount of money.

Now Lisa said, "I need a rubber and has anyone pinched my calculator?" She was the only one of us preparing for school which started on Monday. James would simply throw all his things into his case after breakfast on Monday morning. Ben had put his things ready days ago. He had even cleaned his school shoes. I had washed my school blouses and a skirt, which was shiny with wear. I didn't want to go back to school. The summer had been long and heavenly. Prince had won the Novice Jumping at our local show and come second in the pairs jumping with Lisa on Lorraine. Ben had won a Working Hunter class on Solitaire, who isn't a working hunter, but was the only horse to jump a clear round. Lisa had won numerous Gymkhana events. And I had won the Open Musical Poles at the Pony Club Gymkhana. We had been to the sea. And James had gone to France with a friend called Charles. Dad had done reasonably well selling double glazing, so in spite of the bills dropping through the letter box, we had all had new school blazers except for James who doesn't have to wear one any more. Now going upstairs to find things for school. I thought, it's the lull before the storm. Now we're to lose every-thing – our rooms, our stables, our privacy.

Presently Mum appeared and sat on my bed. "Don't be gloomy Harriet darling," she said. "The time will soon pass. And you may actually like the Abbotts. They *are* horsey after all. You mustn't always look on the black side; it's a bad habit.'

"It's all right, I don't mind giving up my room," I lied looking into Mum's tired face. "Of course I don't. I just hope they're nice. I suppose their horses will have to be stabled. How many are they bringing?"

"Four."

That meant that all the old loose boxes would be occupied, leaving only the two new ones empty. So now I saw our own ponies standing outside waiting to come in as the days grew shorter and the nights colder. Soon they would start neighing and rattling the gates, expecting feeds in their mangers and deep beds of golden straw or pale shavings.

"I feel like a poor relation. I always feel like that when we have children staying," I said going to the window and looking out into the darkness.

"That's a terrible thing to say," replied Mum.

"And where will the dogs sleep?" I cried turning round.

"God knows. We'll have to play it by ear. Oh don't look so glum Harriet. We'll find somewhere for them," Mum said.

But I already knew where that would be. They would sleep in the two remaining loose boxes, the new ones. For they would be that sort of dog, neither small nor sweet as Lisa hoped, but big and expensive, the sort of dogs rich men keep.

"The Abbotts are really very nice darling, I promise you," Mum told me before padding away in knitted sox to console Ben.

At last I had everything ready for school. When I returned on Monday the Abbotts would have arrived. Now I could hear Mum cleaning my real bedroom below. I had emptied the contents of my drawers into suitcases, which were now under the bed in the tiny attic bedroom. I had put my collection of china horses on the window ledge by my bed. Each of them had a name. My favourite books were piled on the bedside table. It was nearly supper time. Next door I found Ben lying on his metal, hospital type bed, staring at the ceiling.

"Once servant girls came here at twelve years old to live in these rooms and to work for Mr and Mrs Black, think of that Harriet," he said.

"Once Ben and Harriet Pemberton were turned out of their rooms and had to sleep up here," I replied. "So what?"

"The Abbotts are rich. Their children will give us their old clothes. Justin will play cricket in white flannels. they'll have rich voices and call us the hoi-poloi," Ben said smiling happily. "But will they change us or us them? That is the question."

"We'll change them," I replied firmly, before going in search of Lisa.

I found her downstairs cleaning her shoes.

"I need a new pair. I need lots of new things. My satchel is held together by safety pins," she complained.

"That's why we are having the Abbotts. As usual we need the money." I said bitterly.

Lisa looked at me through her brown fringe. "But you know we couldn't have the ponies if we didn't have the guests. We would have to live in a tiny house with hardly any garden. Can't you see how lucky we are Harriet!" she cried. And looking at her, so much younger than me and so stoic, made me feel suddenly ashamed.

"But it's all right for you, you don't have to move out of your room," I said.

"But I always live in the attic, that's why. If you did the same it would make life much easier for everyone, and you wouldn't have to move then," replied Lisa.

But I didn't want to live in the attic, because my room looks out onto the paddocks and the stables. It has a big beech tree outside where squirrels swing from branch to branch. It's my room and it always has been, and I love it. It's my lair too and full of memories and dreams and it's been like that almost as long as I can remember."

"I'm looking forward to going back to

school. I want to see Gillian and Rosie again. I shall be in the top form, and Rosie's moving to London after Christmas," Lisa said.

Lisa seemed to be growing older, whereas I felt just the same. I didn't want to grow up. I didn't want to be fourteen or fifteen and never sixteen. I wanted to go on being thirteen for ever.

Monday would be the start of a new year at school with different teachers and different classrooms. And every minute away from Black Pony Inn seemed a minute wasted. I didn't need friends, because I had Ben and Lisa and the ponies. And I would far rather be riding Prince than playing hockey or doing gymnastics in the Gym Hall. I'm being what Dad calls negative, I thought, laying the kitchen table for supper. But I'm going to make myself change. And I vowed that I would stop whinging about my room and like the Abbotts. But I had no idea then how hard it was going to be.

Two
The Abbotts arrive

On Monday when Ben and I returned from school. Lisa met us in the stable yard.

"They've arrived. They came in two posh cars and are drinking tea in the kitchen," she cried.

"You make them sound like an army of occupation," said Ben.

"What about their horses?" I asked.

"They're coming later in a horse box. And guess what, they've got a girl groom. And they absolutely insisted on drinking tea in the kitchen; they said they wanted to be treated as family," Lisa finished.

"Oh God, it gets worse and worse," exclaimed Ben.

"At least they're trying to be friendly," I said.

There was a BMW and a Japanese car parked by the front door. Then Mum saw us and called. "How was school? Come in and meet the Abbotts, instead of lurking out there in the shadows like strangers."

James was examining the cars. Next year he would be leaving school for ever.

A tall man opened the back door and

welcomed us with open arms. "Ah, you must be Harriet," he cried. "I'm so very glad to meet you." He flung his arms around me in a crushing embrace. When he let go, I saw that he had greying hair, a dark moustache and blue eyes. Shaking Ben by the hand he exclaimed, "And you must be Benjamin. I'm glad to meet you too."

A woman who could only be Mrs Abbott, who wore slacks and an expensive jumper with a pattern of dogs on it, said, "Don't be shy Tracey, come and meet Harriet."

Tracey was younger than Lisa. There were gaps between her teeth. When she said, "Hallo," she sounded as though she had a cold.

Justin was dark haired, with a closed expression which gave nothing away. He had a small mouth with tight lips. Looking at Ben now he said, "Your trousers are a bit short aren't they? They really do look most peculiar."

"Oh Justin, what a thing to say! Don't be so rude," cried Mrs Abbott.

"Don't listen to the young pup Ben. Your trousers are fine," said Mr Abbott smiling indulgently.

Ben was looking at his trousers now. he had been wanting a new pair for ages, but hadn't like to ask for one. Now he said, "Ankle length trousers are in fashion, didn't you know Justin? St Peter's *must* be out of date, everyone's wearing them this year."

16

And laughed. Then we heard a horsebox arriving outside and we all rushed out to the stable yard.

A girl was driving the horsebox and the horse-box was towing a caravan.

"Whoa. Stop," shouted Mr Abbott. "That's fine."

Suddenly I wished that Dad was with us, because Mr Abbott seemed to be taking over Black Pony Inn and Mum wasn't stopping him.

"There's a telephone in the BMW. It's very posh," said James joining us.

"So what?" muttered Ben crossly.

Rugged and bandaged with the initials G.A. on their rugs, the horses came down the ramps on the horsebox one by one, each more beautiful than the last.

"Meet Shamus, Sultan, Scorpio and Stardust," said Mrs Abbott proudly.

We had prepared their boxes for them and they were soon installed, while our ponies looked over the field gate, their eyes agog with curiosity. Shamus and Sultan were large bays with beautiful heads and thoroughbred legs. Scorpio was black with one white sock and about fourteen hands. Stardust was about thirteen one, liver chestnut with a small star on his forehead. They were all geldings and beautifully turned out, their coats gleaming, their manes and tails perfoctly pulled, their eyes shining. Looking over the field gate, our ponies suddenly appeared ordinary by comparison, their coats covered with fresh mud from rolling, their manes too long, their fetlocks untrimmed. They looked humble, like poor relations I thought sadly, wiping tears from my eyes.

"What's the matter? Why are you crying?" hissed Lisa.

"I'm not crying stupid. My eyes are watering that's all," I retorted angrily. "I just hate looking at our horses out in the cold, that's all," I added.

"But it isn't cold," replied Lisa missing the point entirely.

The girl groom was large and fair haired. She addressed the Abbotts by their christian names.

"Wow, what a place!" she cried smiling at Lisa as soon as the horses were settled. "Let's see your ponies. Come on I want a proper tour. Are you Lisa?" And I thought that Susan and Lisa seemed to be on the same wave length.

We toured our mud covered ponies. Susan called them all 'poppets'. Mrs Abbott said that Limpet looked like a tinker's pony. They all laughed at Jigsaw's large head and short legs. "His forbears must have been bred for the coal mines," said Mrs Abbott. She called Solitaire 'a good sort', Lorraine a bit light in the neck, Prince she said had character, "Bags of it." Then they showed us their horses in detail, if that is the right word, relating to us the prizes they had won, a whole catalogue of them. After that Tracey asked whether we would like to see her silver cups.

"We can't, we've got our homework to do," said Ben making a face at me. And Justin said, "Have you started school already? St Peter's doesn't start until Wednesday. It's a first class school with people from all over the world."

"I'm sure there are," said James seriously.

I knew St Peter's. It had wrought iron entrance gates with a shield on them. It had a long drive lined with trees, huge playing fields and a lake. It sent crews to regattas and sides to cricket matches. James had once told me that it was full of wimps and that the girls talked as though they had plums in their mouths. So I didn't envy Justin. St Peter's had a preparatory school as well. I had seen tiny children being driven there in school uniforms, and once walking crocodile along a pavement. Poor Tracey, I thought now. I bet it isn't any fun.

"Why don't you come and see our dogs now?" suggested Mrs Abbott, whose blonde hair was swept back, high off her forehead.

The dogs were called Rascal, Ruffian and Ruby. Ruffian was a dobermann, the other two boxers. Ruffian and Ruby were in one of our new loose boxes, Rascal in the other. So now there wasn't a single loose box left for our ponies.

"They win prizes too. Ruffian is a champion," Tracey told us.

"Ruffian isn't his name," said Mr Abbott joining us. "They all have much more complicated names. But it's impossible to call Rednight Ruffian or Roseware Regenade. They are far too long-winded."

Our ponies continued to lean over the field gate, their eyes shining with hope, or was it envy? Or jealousy? Or just plain curiosity? I wished I knew.

At last I went inside to look at Tracey's cups. She had unpacked them and put them on the window-ledge in what I still thought of as my room. There were five, each with her name and the date engraved on it and she gave them to me in turn to look at.

"They're fantastic," I said handing them back one after another.

Her dark blue riding jacket was hanging on a hanger at the end of my bed. A photo of her on a pony bedecked with rosettes was on my chest of drawers.

"I won most of my cups on him," she said pointing at the photograph. "He even went to Wembley. He's called Charcoal Burner. You may have seen his picture in *Horse and Hound*. We called him Burney for short," Tracey explained handing me the photograph.

He was bay and plaited and beautiful. "He's great. But where is he now?" I asked handing it back.

"Sold on. I grew out of him," Tracey said. "Can I see your cups now?"

"I haven't any, only rosettes. But Lisa's got one," I said. And now I felt humiliated, because Tracey seemed to have everything – my room, fame, a girl groom, rich parents. And she was only eight years old! It was almost too much to bear.

"I had better do my homework," I said standing up. "See you." Envy is a sin, I told myself running downstairs. And I've got Prince and he's ten times nicer than all the Abbott horses put together, but I wasn't sure, and I couldn't help imagining myself wearing a dark blue show jacket with a red lining, standing in the middle of the arena at Wembley holding a silver cup.

I helped Mum dish up supper in the kitchen. Dad wasn't home yet. James usually waited on the guests. The sisters, who are called Mrs Tomson and Miss Steele, were always pressing bars of chocolate into his hands. They called him 'our boy'. Miss Steele wore her grey hair short and straight, while Mrs Tomson's was long and in a bun on the back of her head. Miss Steele wore steel spectacles, Mrs Tomson plastic framed ones. They talked alike and were always together. Dad called them the Siamese Twins.

Tracey had supper in her room, sitting up in my bed like a princess. The others ate in the dining room, which is large and pannelled. Justin appeared to be lecturing his parents on computers. The elderly ladies and Colonel Hunter sat at a different table, each with their own table napkin in its own special ring.

While we were putting the dishes in our recently acquired dishwasher, Mum said, "They've parked their caravan behind the stables and Susan is living in it and we haven't got permission."

"Do we have to have it?" I asked.

"Yes of course, we're not a camping site," Mum said.

Ben was cleaning his shoes. "I should let Dad deal with it," he advised, while Lisa interrupted saying, "You're looking for problems, Mum. It'll be all right. I think they're nice and Justin is great. I'm glad they're here. This place was becoming like an old people's home." And now we could hear Colonel Hunter talking. He was telling the Abbotts about his wartime experiences which had been the highlight of his life.

It was like any other evening, but different because the Abbotts were with us, which made Mum on edge, as she always is with new guests, for she's afraid they'll find the beds hard or the food not to their liking. She hates guests complaining. One complaint and her day is ruined.

I went upstairs to fetch Tracey's tray. She was reading *Pony* with a teddy bear beside her. "I love this room, it's so comfy," she said smiling at me, wanting to be liked, while I only saw a spoilt little girl in my bed, with half the food uneaten on her plate.

"Yes, it's the nicest room in the house," I answered bitterly, taking her tray.

"And the bed's lovely and soft," she added as I shut the door after me.

I cannot remember how that particular day ended. I remember I did my homework in the playroom using oceans of Tipp-Ex, and I remember lying in bed looking at the eaves in my attic without seeing them, seeing instead myself at a huge horse show with television cameras looking down on me and the Queen in the Royal Box.

"We've had so many guests, I can't think why you're whinging about the Abbotts, Harriet," said Ben next morning as we waited for the school bus. "They aren't any trouble and having a basin and shower instead of a bathroom isn't the end of the world. I know you don't like giving up your bedroom – but there are people who don't have a bedroom, who sleep on pavements, or on the floor in mud huts."

"Thanks for the social lecture. But I know you're only trying to convince yourself, because you care as much as I do," I replied with unusual perception. And I saw that I was right, because as I spoke Ben wiped a tear from one of his large hazel coloured eyes.

That day at school seemed no more than an interlude between being with and being away from the Abbotts. Mr Abbott had left for London at 5 a.m. in his BMW. Dad had risen early to give him breakfast, then left himself in our ancient Volvo. Miss Steele and Mrs Tomson had had breakfast on the stroke of eight in the dining room. I know because James overslept, so I had waited on them and remember them saying "Where's our boy then?" The rest of the day seemed endless. But at last we were climbing into the school bus again, which goes miles around the countryside dropping pupils off at remote villages before leaving us on the edge of the common.

When we reached home at last it was to find Tracey riding round and round our small paddock on Stardust. She was cantering circles, then popping Stardust over our one and only cavalettii, Mrs Abbott was watching.

Seeing us, she called, "Halt," in a loud voice. Then beckoning to us she added, "You'll have to get some more poles and uprights, Harriet. What's here is totally inadequate."

"We have a few more poles and some oil drums somewhere," answered Ben vaguely. "And some cross country fences if you look."

"Your mother doesn't seem to know anything about the horses. She says it's your business," grumbled Mrs Abbott, who was beautifully dressed in barbour, elegant slacks, smart boots and a deerstalker. But whatever she wore, she would always look wonderful, I thought enviously, admiring her slim figure.

"I'll find you a pole," offered Ben handing me his school case.'

"I need more than one, six at least," she shouted back in a voice used to being obeyed.

It seemed to be Susan's day off, for as we searched for poles we could hear music coming from her caravan. I can't remember what it was now, except that it was loud and modern, the sort of thing James listens to with his girl friend Virginia. At last we found some poles lying in a bed of nettles.

"I'll just take off my school clothes, then I'll be right back," Ben shouted.

"Mrs Abbott didn't ask us whether Tracey could ride in our paddock. And now she's cutting it up," I grumbled, following Ben indoors.

Lisa was sitting in the kitchen stuffing crumpets. "She wants poles," she said.

"Who's she? The cat's mother?" I asked.

"Tracey rides every day after school. She hasn't a single friend. She says she doesn't need them. She's too busy," continued Lisa talking through a half eaten crumpet.

"Lucky her. Where's Justin then?" I asked, taking off my blazer.

"Tacking up. He says that either you do things professionally and with dedication or not at all. His school motto is: *Dedication Breeds Excellence* – in Latin of course. It's on his blazer," said Lisa.

"And on the school gates. When do they start school anyway?" I asked.

"Tomorrow. They've been buying things for school today," said Lisa, starting to eat yet another crumpet.

We returned to the stable yard. Justin was schooling by himself in the bottom paddock, riding round and round on black Scorpio. Ben and I dragged the poles to the schooling paddock. I stung my hands, while one of the dogs chased our cat Twinkle to the top of a tall tree. Our ponies stood watching the schooling session like spectators at a cricket match.

"I think I prefer old ladies. They don't want poles, or to cut up our paddock, or use all our loose boxes," I said.

"You sound like an old person yourself, grumble, grumble," retorted Ben.

We watched Tracey schooling Stardust. Mrs Abbott was still standing in the centre of the paddock like an instructor. "Shorten your reins, keep contact. That's it, well done, steady, steady, don't let him lose cadence. I want you to lengthen his stride Tracey. That's it. Well done." Then she turned to us and called, "Why don't you ride with Tracey, Harriet?"

"Go on, show what you can do," urged Ben.

So I caught Prince and, after brushing him quickly with a dandy brush, tacked him up. Ben held my stirrup while I mounted.

"Go on, you show them," he said again,

smiling in a silly way as he opened the paddock gate to let me through.

"Do up the harness on your hat Harriet,"
called Mrs Abbott. "That's better. Now let's
see how you're sitting," she continued pushing me in the back. "Of course your saddle
doesn't help. You need a deep-seated one."
she added after a moment.

"And isn't she riding too short Mummy?"
asked Tracey in her bossy little voice, which
I was beginning to hate.

"Yes, you're absolutely right poppet, she
is," said Mrs Abbott warmly. "Now come on,
Harriet, hang your legs down, stretch, that's
better. You young people never realize that
you grow. You go on and on riding with the
same length of stirrup. It's crazy. Two
notches down I think. How does that look
Tracey?" she asked.

"Okay Mummy, much better."

"Thank you poppet."

Ben was leaning on the gate splitting his
sides with laughter.

"Okay Harriet, off you go now on the right
rein. Keep contact. Legs further back. Oh
dear, oh dear, your leg position is still out
of tune Harriet," she called standing in the
middle now. "Halt. I want to show you
something."

And that's how it went on. Stop, start.
Tracey's advice and comments treated like
pearls of wisdom by Mrs Abbott. Ben grew
tired and went indoors. Dusk darkened the

sky. Susan emerged from the caravan. Justin put the dogs to bed. But I had to admit that Mrs Abbott was a marvellous instructor and soon Prince was dropping his nose and relaxing his back and feeling wonderful. It was Tracey who spoilt the lesson because she couldn't help adding her comments all the time. Things like: "She isn't looking ahead Mummy," and "Shouldn't she change her diagonal now Mummy?"

Justin and Scorpio joined us briefly towards the end. "Now darling show Harriet how a circle should be done," Mrs Abbott said. "Now watch Harriet. See how Scorpio bends his body. Prince can't do that yet, he's too stiff. Asking him to make a circle is like asking a pencil, neither of them can bend. Harriet, are you listening?"

I nodded. I knew she was right, they were all right. But I was finding it hard to take, especially from eight year old Tracey.

As we untacked in the yard Tracey said, "Don't worry Harriet. Prince will improve in time. I know he will."

"Lungeing will help," Justin advised. But you must keep up your schooling. Riding once or twice a week isn't good enough, not if you want to win anyway." And he sounded at least twenty years old.

"And you know you haven't won a single cup yet Harriet. Wouldn't you like a row of them like me?" asked Tracey smiling into my face.

Three
"Where's Tracey?"

I tried to like the Abbotts. We all did. They
paid Lisa to exercise their dogs after school.
Tracey followed me everywhere, often she sat
on my bed simply staring at me. Mum said
that she had a pash on me, poor thing. Tracey
even wanted me to watch television with her
every evening on the set she had now in what
I still considered my bedroom. And the more
she liked me, the more of a hypocrite I felt.

Susan pulled our horses' manes and tails
without asking and free of charge, which
upset Ben who thinks long manes are roman-
tic, and me because I was afraid they would
be cold living outside without them. But we
said, "How lovely," and "Thank you," all the
same.

Susan chatted up James and invited him
into her caravan, which wasn't any tidier
than his room, being full of clothes thrown
down everywhere and dirty mugs in the
small sink. But James had his girl friend
Virginia already and wasn't interested in
Susan. He only went into the caravan out
of politeness. Mr Abbott worked incredible
hours and we hardly saw him. James called

29

him a "worker bee". Mrs Abbott rode their horses every morning with Susan. It turned out that she was a qualified instructor. She advised me to change Prince's bit and took away the martingale he had been wearing. She expected me to be absolutely dedicated to riding, all the time. "That's the only way you'll succeed." she told me. So what with Tracey's demands and so much riding, I never had a moment to myself.

When Justin wasn't riding or at school he played chess on his computer, which was now in Ben's old room. Otherwise he watched television programmes, but only the ones which taught him something like Block-busters. He knew so many facts that Ben dubbed him a walking encyclopaedia. "Don't any of them ever day-dream?" he asked, when for a moment we were alone leaning on a field gate, sucking blades of autumn grass. "Or stop to look at a sun-set? And all this riding to win, I know it's important, but what about life being fun as well," he continued. "I don't believe they've ever played charades, or any game which isn't in some way educational. I don't believe that Justin has ever been young."

"But he'll be famous, while we're nonentit-ies," I countered.

"If he doesn't crack up first," replied Ben.

Mum had taken on an extra cleaning lady to cope with the Abbotts. She was called Peggy and had always lost her dusters or the polish. And I could see that she annoyed the Abbotts. "Why doesn't she get her act together?" demanded Mrs Abbott one day.

"Perhaps she hasn't got an act," I said.

"No wonder she's only a cleaning woman then," Mrs Abbott continued. "I've no patience with that sort of person. She needs to pull her socks up. Shall I speak to her?"

"No thank you, she'll leave if you do," I said quickly. "Mum says that praise is the best spur. Anyway, no one wants to clean other people's houses these days; they think it's demeaning."

"Well, if they can't do anything else, they have no choice,' snapped Mrs Abbott.

The leaves were changing colour on the trees. Soon it would be to dark to ride after school. What would the Abbotts do then? I wondered. If Tracey had a pash on me, Lisa had one on Susan, for now she spent every spare moment in the caravan playing cards with Susan or trying on her make-up. At weekends she helped Susan instead of looking after our horses. It was, "Susan says this," or "Susan says that," all day long until I felt like screaming. And when she wasn't with Susan, she was exercising Rascal, Ruffian and Ruby, keeping them on their leads, dragging them around the common in the dusk. Soon she was hardly ever in the house, so that Mum told her that she was treating it like a hotel. James spent all his spare time with Virginia, who was red haired and rather snooty. Our horses meanwhile continued to look over the gate at the stables every evening, while I started to pray that the Abbotts would be gone before the cold weather arrived, for I desperately wanted life to be normal by Christmas.

Comparing this time with what was to come after, it was a quiet time. And at least Lisa was happy, for she was being paid five pounds a week for exercising the dogs and had already bought herself stripey socks with the money and a red woolly hat.

Our troubles really began on the day Tracey asked whether she might ride with me. "Please, please. I won't be a nuisance, I promise," she pleaded watching me tack up Prince.

I didn't want her. I wanted to ride alone. I love riding alone. There was a little whispering breeze now which picked up the bits of the hay lying in the yard and whisked them away. The first leaves were falling off the trees, just a few, nothing like the avalanche which would follow in a few weeks' time.

"Must you? Well, you had better ask your mother then," I replied without enthusiasm, hoping her mother would say no.

"Thank you, oh thank you Harriet," cried Tracey running towards the house to find her mother.

I pulled up Prince's girths and let down my stirrups. And now I was sure Mrs Abbott would refuse, because she wouldn't trust me, wouldn't believe I was capable of looking after Tracey. But a minute later Tracey was back, her glowing face relaying the news before she even opened her mouth to cry, "I can go. She said yes."

Susan tacked up Stardust, saying glumly, "Rather you than me Harriet. And you'll have to see to him when you get back. I'm off this afternoon. It is Saturday you know. And I have to have a half day off sometimes."

"That's all right. I'll see to him, not to worry," I said Prince was on edge. He didn't like Stardust. And it seemed ages since I had ridden him out.

"We'll go through the woods. Are you sure you'll be all right?" I asked Tracey as Susan put her up, tightening her girths and adjusting her stirrups. Tracey nodded; she was still glowing with happiness which made me think, she's really rather sweet and at least, she doesn't argue all the time like Lisa.

Stardust had to jog to keep up with Prince who has a wonderful walk. Tracey's face was creased with happiness. I was surprised her Mum hadn't appeared to see us off. Stardust wore a kimblewick bit and was afraid of his mouth. He looked at everything – pieces of paper, manholes in the road, dustbins left outside houses. But soon we were in the woods which held so many memories for me. In spring there is a carpet of bluebells under the tall beech trees there. Today there was a coating of orange leaves which rustled beneath our horses' hoofs. We trotted on and Tracey was still smiling. "I've never hacked like this before Harriet. It's lovely," she told me.

And suddenly I was afraid. I slowed down. "We'd better walk then," I said. "We don't want you to do too much the first time, do we?"

But Tracey wanted to trot. It's quite different to riding in the school with Mummy in the middle," she chirped happily. "I feel really grown up riding with you Harriet. 'It's super duper."

We came out of the wood and rode down a lane. Then we reached the last of the year's stubble, which in a week's time would become dark ploughed earth. "Are you all right for a canter?" I asked. "Just a slow one, nothing fast."

Tracey nodded, her hat pushed low on her forehead. We smiled at one another, and she gave a happy giggle as we set off gently side by side. "It's lovely Harriet," she said again.

Prince was going well, he had dropped his nose and his hocks were under him. He felt as though he could go for ever. The wind blew gently in our faces. The sky was full of dancing clouds. It was a spring day in autumn, that's how it felt anyway.

I saw dogs in the distance and then, without warning, a gun went off and then another and another, and now Stardust was galloping with Tracey screaming on top.

34

I shouted, "Sit up, sit back, pull on the reins Tracey." But with an awful feeling in the pit of my stomach I knew that nothing would stop Stardust now. His head was down and he was heading for home. And if I chased him he would simply go faster and faster, so with my heart hammering, I cantered behind calling out instructions, while fear invaded my stomach and my brain felt clear and icy cold with an awful fatalism.

I could see the men now with their guns. There were three of them and were carrying dead pigeons. Stardust had reached the end of the stubble now and was back in the woods, and I could hear Tracey calling, "I can't stop him Harriet." It was a moment I would never forget, which would be engraved forever in my memory, so that I would never gallop on stubble again without recalling it with horror. I pushed Prince into a gallop. I reached the wood, but the faster I went, the faster Stardust galloped. It was the old quandary. Chase a horse and you'll send him faster, stay behind, and with luck he'll stop and wait for you. Only Stardust wasn't stopping. And he had no intention of waiting for me. Stardust was heading for home and I knew that in a minute he was going to be galloping down a road full of Saturday shoppers driving into town. Then he was going to sprint across the common and swing into the stable yard at a flat out gallop. And there was nothing I could do to stop him.

It was then that I started to pray, "God please help Tracey, please make Stardust stop." But since I never go to church I could hardly expect God to do anything, and He didn't.

When I reached the road, several cars had already stopped. Stardust was disappearing into the distance and a young couple were kneeling over Tracey. I drew rein then, my heart hammered with fear, while Prince threw his head up and down with impatience. I dismounted before I approached the couple. "Is she all right?" I asked nervously.

"Yes poor kid, but her mouth is full of blood," the woman said.

I imagined Tracey toothless, her parents wrath. And at that moment I wished that the earth would swallow me up.

Then Tracey stood up; her face was covered with a mixture of mud, tears and blood. "He wouldn't stop. I pulled and pulled. I really did Harriet," she said.

"He's a beastly pony who should be shot," I answered.

"We'll take you home dear. Where is it?" the woman asked. I could see that they were a nice couple. He with dark hair and she with fair. They were nicely dressed too. James would have called them yuppies. Tracey pointed to a Black Pony Inn standing beyond the common, old and turretted in parts. The woman helped Tracey into their car, while I set off for home at a gallop.

There was a crowd waiting by the yard gate.

"Where's Tracey?" screamed Mrs Abbott.

"What's happened?" asked Mum looking at me frantically.

Ben was holding Stardust. He had scraped one knee, otherwise he appeared unhurt.

"She's all right. She can walk and everything," I said lamely.

"How dare you take her out without permission?" shouted Mrs Abbott.

"But Tracey asked you. I know she did." I dismounted and my legs felt weak and my head was still fuzzy with fright.

"She didn't ask. She just said, could she ride with you. That's all Harriet. She isn't good enough to ride Stardust out," said Mrs Abbott.

"Any fool can see that," added Justin spitefully.

Lisa was crying. Was she sorry for me or for Tracey I wondered? The car was turning into the yard now. The young woman, who seemed to be called Margaret, jumped out. "Your little girl threw herself off when she saw the cars. She could have been killed," she said.

I saw now that Tracey had grazed her chin. She looked pale and grimey and shocked all at the same time.

"I couldn't stop him Mummy," she said. "There were guns. Men shooting. It was horrible."

I felt so ashamed now that I couldn't look at anyone. Feeling like an outcast I untacked Prince, while Ben saw to Stardust. "It was my fault wasn't it? But Tracey was always telling me how to ride so I thought she was an expert. I must have been brainwashed," I muttered.

"You wait until Mr Abbott gets home," replied Ben darkly.

When I had turned out Prince, I went upstairs and into my own bedroom without thinking. But of course it was full of Tracey's things, so I went to the attic and sat on my bed and cried.

Presently Mum joined me. "Don't sulk Harriet, these things will happen. Time passes and they are forgotten," she said.

I looked at her face. "Why can't they just go," I replied. "They aren't our sort of people. They're so competitive and they think they know everything and I *mean everything*. And I was just beginning to like Tracey," I added and started to cry harder than ever.

"Oh Harriet you are too big for tears," Mum said.

"There's nothing nice about them," I continued wiping my eyes. "Mrs Abbott's a bully. She bullies everyone. And the children have to win, it's win, win, all the time. I know I haven't a single silver cup but I don't care."

"It takes all kinds to make a world. It's lunch in half an hour Harriet,' said Mum getting off my bed. "Wash your face and your hair – please."

I didn't go down to lunch. Lisa brought me some stew on a plate. "Tracey's got a black eye and she's probably cracked a front tooth. You *are* in the dog-house now Harriet," she said. "You must have been mad to gallop towards home on Mr Brind's stubble. Even I wouldn't have been so stupid."

And now I hated Lisa too.

Later there was a knock on my bedroom door. "Come in," I cried hastily straightening my duvet, then wiping my eyes.

It was Mr Abbott. He said, "We *are* disappointed in you Harriet. We never thought you would be so foolish, or so devious." He was wearing a suit and a gold watch on a hairy wrist and suede shoes. I wasn't sure what devious meant.

"We trusted you. We didn't think you would hurt our little girl," he continued.

"I didn't. She fell off. We all fall off sometimes," I answered. "It's inevitable. Anyway Stardust is too much for her. She's too small for him."

"Exactly," agreed Mr Abbott looking at me. "That's why you shouldn't have taken her out."

I didn't know what to say. I felt all sorts of things – humiliation, defeat, frustration, but most of all guilt. "She did ask. It was a misunderstanding. I wouldn't have taken her out if she hadn't asked your wife. I'm not that silly," I answered. "I never take children out riding without their parents' permission, not even Lisa's friends. It's a rule here."

And now I felt quite calm for I knew what I was saying was true. Quite suddenly I didn't feel guilty any more.

"She'll have to have her front teeth crowned or capped when she's older and her nerves are all to pieces," continued Mr Abbott.

But I could look at him now. He had brown eyes and suddenly I knew he had been sent by Mrs Abbott to tell me off, and he wasn't enjoying it.

"Ben has a crowned tooth. He broke it when he was a toddler. But no one knows or notices. Mum says you can't get through life without a few dents," I said. "Unless of course you never do anything exciting ever. And what sort of life is that Mr Abbott?" I finished.

"A boring one," he said beginning to laugh in spite of himself. "Well don't do it again Harriet," he added with a hint of a smile.

"No way. I'm not a complete idiot," I answered quickly.

He shut my door after him. I hoped that would be the end of it, but of course it wasn't. Mrs Abbott avoided me. And now Tracey only rode Stardust on a lunge rein. And whatever anyone had said, I knew that I was still blamed for what had happened, though I also knew it wasn't all my fault.

Four
"It's fate"

Things were to grow worse for the next evening Lisa came flying into the kitchen shouting, "I've lost Rascal. He slipped his collar and he's gone. I called and called. He'll get run over I know he will, and the Abbotts will never forgive me."

I was trying to do my maths homework. Ben was reading again. Outside it was growing dark.

"He's the big one isn't he?" Ben asked. "The one with white down his front."

"He's the boxer." Tears were streaming down Lisa's face. "The most valuable one. The Abbotts will kill me, I know they will," she screamed.

Luckily the Abbotts had gone shopping, except for Mr Abbott who was away working as usual. They had taken Susan with them.

"I'll look on Prince," I offered. "I'll get some string and lead him back. I'll find him."

"And I'll look on my bike," Ben said.

"But it hasn't got any lights," I shouted.

"Who cares? You haven't anyway, unless you call Prince's eyes lights," replied Ben laughing.

We rushed outside. I caught Prince, tacked him up, and remembered my hat. Then I was gone galloping in the dusk across a rain sodden common. I went straight to the woods. I drew rein there and called, "Rascal, Rascal. Come here Rascal." Then I tried whistling. But the only answer was from the dripping trees. Drip, drip, drip. I rode on remembering that I had left no message, told no one where I was going, not even James. And as I rode, I cursed the Abbotts again. They've brought us nothing but misery I thought. Surely they realise that dogs need taking out more than once a day by poor Lisa, who has hours of homework to do every evening, who shouldn't be walking them at all. Then I thought that all the money in the world wasn't worth what we were going through. After that I talked to Prince. "They'll soon be gone," I told him, "then you'll have your own lovely loose box back again. You won't have to live out any more in the wet and the cold." He put back an ear and listened to me. And the trees went on dripping and there was no sign of Rascal anywhere. I halted Prince and called again and again, "Rascal, Rascal, come here good dog." And the tall, wet trees seemed to swallow up my voice and stifle it. "I'm sorry, Lisa, but there it is," I said to myself. "It's your turn to be in the dog-house now!"

I turned and galloped back through the woods and across the common. And now the houses there had their lights on glimmering in the murky dusk. I didn't want to go home. Already I was imagining the row – Lisa screaming, Mrs Abbott instructing everyone as though we were all kids at her special school for delinquents. Justin smug and self-righteous. Tracey standing behind her mother not knowing what to say, because, in spite of everything, she still liked me and Lisa. It isn't anybody's fault, I thought, riding across the common. It's fate. But Mrs Abbott will have to blame someone, she always does.

When I returned to the yard everything was unusually quiet. I turned Prince out and wiped my boots on some long grass before I went indoors. There was no sign of Lisa or Ben; just James reading Hamlet at the kitchen table.

"Where's everybody?" I asked nervously.

"Gone to see a vet. The Abbotts are still shopping. Rascal's been run over," explained James without looking up from Hamlet.

"I don't believe it!" I cried.

"Ben found him. He caused an accident. Two cars bumped into one another. Mum had to sort it out. Lisa just screamed and screamed as usual," James continued drinking tea out of a mug.

"Is Rascal going to die?" I asked.

"I shouldn't think so. His eyes were open anyway," James answered.

"I think I shall hide somewhere because I

don't want to see Mrs Abbott and have to explain," I said after a moment.

"Good thinking," said James. "She thinks I'm dotty, so she won't ask me anything."

"Sometimes I just wish they would all die," I said.

James looked at me in disbelief. "You don't mean that do you? You can't," he said.

"Not really, but half of me does. I want everything to be as it was before they came. It was so peaceful then," I said.

"Only by comparison," James answered.

Then we both saw car lights approaching. I ducked under the kitchen table and held my breath.

"I had better got their tea. I'll make them buttered toast and there's some chocolate cake," said James putting down his book.

"Don't speak to me. I'm not here," I hissed, pulling the table cloth towards the floor so that they shouldn't see me.

But it wasn't the Abbotts. It was Mum, Ben, Lisa and Rascal. Feeling stupid I crawled out from under the table.

"What are you doing there?" Mum asked.

"Hiding from the Abbotts," I said laughing.

To my surprise Lisa wasn't crying. "Rascal's all right. He's only suffering from shock," she said. "But I don't suppose I'll be allowed to walk the dogs any more, and I did like the fiver every week. Now I'll be poor again."

Mum made a bed with pillows and a

blanket by the Aga for Rascal. "He's had a sedative," she told me. "I hope Mrs Abbott understands. I'm going to ring the insurance company about the cars. Don't do anything silly meantime. Let me deal with Mrs Abbott, do you hear Lisa?"

Lisa nodded. "I wish they would go away and never come back," she said.

"Same here," I added.

"Same here," said Miss Steele holding out a hot-water bottle to be filled.

Ben filled the hot-water bottle while I laid the table for tea. James returned to Hamlet. Rascal was snoring by the Aga. But though we behaved normally, we were all on edge waiting for the row to begin!

Justin was the first to appear. He rushed into the kitchen; then stopped dead in his tracks. "What's he doing there?" he asked pointing to Rascal. "He should be outside."

I looked at Rascal and I must say he did look sweet wrapped in a pink blanket with his head resting on a blue pillow. He looked like a dog which is loved, instead of a show dog locked in a kennel half his life.

"He's had a little accident," said James smiling at Justin. "But as you can see, he's all right now. He was a little shocked, hence the pink blanket. But he's going to be all right."

Mrs Abbott was wearing a shiny mackintosh with a fur collar. She put down her shopping on the kitchen table, just as though it was her house. Then she looked at James with dislike. "What about tea? We're famished," she said.

Justin pointed to Rascal. "Haven't you noticed Mummy? Rascal's had an accident," he said, and he might have added, "And who's to blame? There must be a culprit," — for I swear that was what he was thinking. I thought then that he would make a good prosecutor and I could see him condemning people to life imprisonment. He would enjoy it.

"Oh no, what's happened now?" asked Mrs Abbott. "And who's responsible? Why isn't Rascal outside with the others? He's worth a lot of money you know. When we're settled we mean to use him as a stud dog." (Everything the Abbotts owned was worth a lot of money. They only bought the best, you see.)

"He escaped. He slipped his collar, but he's all right," James said calmly, as though dogs slipped their collars and caused accidents every day.

"It was my fault. He wriggled out of his collar. He's been to the vet. He's been X rayed. And we will pay for everything," said Lisa recklessly.

Mrs Abbott took off her beautiful mackintosh and, kneeling on the floor, looked at Rascal. "You were lucky this time Lisa. But I don't think you had better walk the dogs any more," she said getting up. "You're not up to it."

And thinking of the five pounds a week, Lisa wiped tears from her eyes. "I can manage the others," she said. "They are never any trouble."

But Mrs Abbott merely shook her head. "We'll have to pay Susan extra to walk them Lisa. I'm sorry, but there it is. We let you try and you failed us, so that's that," she said.

So, no second chances I thought. Poor Lisa. No more stripey socks or treats for Lorraine. Lisa was looking out of the windows, where the curtains hadn't been drawn, and I knew she was crying. And I thought I'm crying too inside, but no one can see my tears.

Rascal loved being in the kitchen. Next day he had to be dragged outside by his collar and pushed forcefully into his loose box. Susan glared at Lisa. "So I've got to look after them now," she said. "Why didn't you hang on to him, you idiot?"

"But you're being paid for it," said Justin. "So you should be grateful. You'll have a nice little nest-egg by and by. You'll be able to buy a fantastic wedding dress with it."

"Speak for yourself," retorted Susan. "I spend all I get. I need to. I'll never have a nest-egg. And I don't want a fantastic wedding dress, thank you."

Our horses were already growing thick winter coats for the cold months which lay ahead. Normally by this time they would have been in at night contentedly munching hay out of hay nets. When I complained about it Mum said, "Oh Harriet, just keep thinking of the swimming pool." But I'm not a keen swimmer. I would rather be riding, so it wasn't much consolation.

There was nothing to tell us then of what lay ahead that Friday morning. Just the usual friction between us and the Abbotts which seemed to spoil each day. Before I went for the school bus next day, I fed our horses. Lisa and James had already left. Ben had gone ahead to meet a friend. The horses blew hot breath into my hair. The hay smelt wonderful. Susan was mucking out, her fair hair hidden by a head scarf. "You'll be late for school," she called, and then, "There's hay in your hair, Harriet."

Ignoring her I ran for the school bus. I was only just in time. The back seat was full of pushing boys.

"There's hay in your hair, Harriet," someone said.

"And stuck to your socks," laughed a first year.

"Your shoes are muddy," said Rosemary, whom no one likes because she's so fat, poor thing.

"I don't care," I said and meant it.

School dragged. But there wasn't the whisper of a breeze as I boarded the bus for home that evening, absolutely nothing to warn us of what lay ahead.

Ben was sitting at the back with a boy called Dave. It was still light, light enough to feed the horses when I got home if Lisa hadn't done it already. And tomorrow was Saturday.

The bus stopped to let pupils out and I thought, I'll go for a long ride tomorrow, for hours and hours. Perhaps Lisa will be nice and come with me, or Ben. But even if they don't, I'll take sandwiches and go for the day. I'll take a map and find new bridleways. And I saw myself riding on and on, down long lanes. I saw myself galloping, perhaps popping over an odd fence if no one was looking. I was beginning to feel really cheerful by the time we reached home. Our horses were waiting to be fed again. There was no sign of Lisa. I fetched feeds then hay. A wind picked up wisps of hay and carried them away. Clouds were racing each other in a darkening sky. The leaves left on the trees quivered. The dead elms were bare as skeletons against the evening sky. I fetched my tack and took it inside to clean. I told Mum of my plan for the morrow.

"Try to get someone to go with you. I hate you going so far on your own. Anything could happen," she said.

"But I always try to tell you where I'm going," I replied.

That evening is engraved on my memory for ever. Dad came in late looking disheartened. Justin had an argument with Ben. I helped Lisa with her homework. She wasn't doing very well at school and her end of the

year report had been bad. James rang up
Virginia and talked for half an hour. The
elderly ladies were both knitting in the sitting room. Colonel Hunter was watching
television with a glass of whisky and soda
beside him.

At nine-thirty it started to rain. I know
the time because I was setting my alarm
clock for seven-thirty the next morning. My
curtains were drawn back and, looking at the
falling rain, I thought Prince's back will be
wet, too wet to ride tomorrow, so I shan't be
able to go, and I felt like screaming with
disappointment.

Then I heard Mr Abbott coming back from
work. He was laughing and talking about
a deal. He called for champagne, but Dad
couldn't provide him with any.

Later I lay in bed listening to the rain
lashing the window panes, and again I kept
thinking of our horses outside in it, and I
started to hate the Abbotts all over again.

And then at last I slept.

Five
The hurricane

It was a terrible dream. Tracey was disappearing into the distance on Stardust all over again. But now his hoofs were clattering on tarmac.

Then there was the sound of a train rushing faster and faster towards Stardust, while Tracey let out an ear-splitting scream and Mrs Abbott called, "It's all right poppet. It's only a storm." Next there was a sound like paper tearing and now I knew that it wasn't just a dream – most of it was real. I leapt out of bed. My window was rattling as though the devil himself was trying to get inside. Mrs Abbott was talking to Tracey below in my real bedroom. I drew back my curtains which jumped and jerked spurred by the wind coming through the window panes, as though they had a life of their own. Outside dawn was breaking, a wild tempestuous dawn with clouds riding the sky like galleons on a tempestuous sea. Branches were flying across the drive as though possessed by demons. A pine tree lay split down the centre on the gravel. The bay trees which normally stand outside the back door in pots had vanished. And there was a wild moon which vanished now leaving me in total darkness. I switched on the light and called out to Ben. "Are you awake? Wake up. Come and look."

Then there was a tremendous crash and all the lights went out.

"The horses! What about the horses?" shouted Ben from next door as I fumbled my way to the door.

Now Ben was emerging from his bedroom. Lisa was screaming, "What's going on? Is there a war or something?"

"It's a hurricane," cried Ben who always has an answer. "And it's throwing trees about like ninepins. Listen! There goes a chimney pot."

"How do you know it's a chimney pot?" I asked crossly, because Ben seemed to be enjoying himself while my teeth were chattering, half in fright, half cold.

"Can't you hear the clatter of bricks falling?" he asked. We were all on the landing now and we could hear the guests talking in excited voices downstairs. Colonel Hunter was walking about guided by a lighted match. Tracey was shrieking. Dad was shouting, "No one is to go outside. Do you hear? No one!"

"I'll make some tea," offered James. "I take it the Aga is still working?"

Someone had found a torch.

"What about the horses?" I asked entering

the kitchen. "We can't just leave them to their fate. We must do something."

"There's nothing we can do, not until the wind stops. Listen, there goes another tree," Dad said.

"But . . ." I began, as my imagination started to run riot, seeing horses crushed to death, the stables in a heap, blood and confusion everywhere.

"No buts, Harriet. Your Father's right; you'll only get killed by a fallen tree, and that won't help anyone, least of all the horses," said Mr Abbott.

Miss Steele appeared now. "I had to feel my way downstairs, there's all sorts of stuff coming down my chimney. I can't stop there, it isn't safe," she said talking in a funny way because she wasn't wearing her false teeth. Then Mum drew back the kitchen curtains and we saw that dawn was breaking, a wild, mad dawn.

We could see each other now: Colonel Hunter in an ancient red dressing gown and leather slippers; Miss Steele and Mrs Tomson in thick nighties which reached to their feet talking to one another about a war of long ago when London burned, and they picked up the bits. Mrs Abbott was there too wearing a wonderful dressing gown with peacocks on it. Mr Abbott was in silk pyjamas and a turquoise towelling dressing gown. Justin was in nothing but pyjamas and shivering. Tracey was in pyjamas with an anorak over

53

them, Mum and Dad had dressed, but Mum's pullover was on back-to-front and Dad was wearing different coloured socks. James was in a striped pyjama top and trousers and Ben wore much the same; while I was still in pyjamas and, as we sipped tea out of mugs, slowly day broke outside, revealing a terrible picture of destruction and devastation.

Mr Abbott pulled open the back door. And, above the noise of the wind, we could hear him shouting, "We can't get out, there's a tree down. Has anyone got a chain saw?"

"No, it's broken," Dad shouted back, before, with one accord, we rushed towards the front door. Ben pulled it open. Mrs Abbott's car was upside down. The front gate had gone. There were fallen trees everywhere, trees I had loved. Suddenly it seemed like the end of the world. And then the wind unexpectedly stopped roaring. I rushed for boots and a coat with Lisa close behind me. "Our poor horses," I shouted.

"Yes. They may be dead, squashed to bits," shouted Lisa rushing outside, struggling into her boots as she ran.

The roof and one wall had gone from the modern loose boxes and the Abbotts' dogs had gone too.

"They can't blame me this time. Oh God what are we going to do? What's happened?" shouted Lisa.

We stopped and stared. The caravan was upside down, and there was no sound coming from it. Then Lisa yelled, "Susan! Susan! Are you all right?"

And now Mr and Mrs Abbott were close behind us. "Leave this to us," said Mr Abbott and knelt down by the caravan, his grey hair blowing in all directions. "She's there. She's unconscious but she's there," he said after a second. "Someone telephone for a doctor. Hurry up." I rushed indoors, my boots leaving a trail of mud and debris behind me. "We need a doctor," I screamed.

James picked up the telephone. Then he shouted, "It's dead. Everything's dead."

"What are we going to do then?" I screamed. "Susan could be dying. And now we won't be able to get a vet either."

"We're on our own," replied James. "We will have to cope."

When I returned to the caravan it had been turned over and Mr and Mrs Abbott were lifting Susan out.

"I can't get a doctor, the telephone doesn't work," I said helplessly.

Susan looked pale and there was blood on her fair hair.

"We'll take her into the house. Keep away from the trees," advised Mrs Abbott.

'Is she going to die?" asked Lisa who is always expecting the worst to happen.

"No, she's not," snapped Mrs Abbott. "And don't stand there staring. Get a blanket and a hot-water bottle."

For a moment we forgot all about our

horses. I rushed back to the house again, climbing over fallen branches on the way. James filled a hot-water bottle. Mum found a blanket. We laid Susan on the sofa in the sitting room. Lisa was crying. "I really liked her. She was my best friend," she sobbed.

"Don't be ridiculous. She's not going to die. Pull your socks up. Stop blubbering Lisa," thundered Mrs Abbott.

"How do you know she isn't going to die? She may have internal injuries," Lisa replied still crying.

"Because I'm a trained nurse, that's why."

We left Susan and returned outside. A huge sycamore tree had fallen across the field shelter. Our first pony, Limpet was inside and whinnied anxiously.

"He'll be all right for the moment," called Mrs Abbott. "Let's look at the others. Leave him there. Do as I say. I know what I'm talking about."

A huge branch had blown into Shamus' box and he was cowering at the back of it, one leg streaked with blood. "Steady there, steady there old boy, whoa, steady," Mrs Abbott slipped quietly into the box.

"Is he going to bleed to death? What about a torniquet?" I asked anxiously watching his bed of shavings slowly turning red.

"Get a stable bandage from the tack room and some wadding. Hurry!" said Mrs Abbott.

I ran. Justin was calling from inside

another loose box. "Stardust is lying down Mummy. I think he's hurt."

Lisa joined him. I could hear Prince neighing from the field. Then Mum appeared with a bucket of warm water and antiseptic. "Thank you. But we don't need it yet. I've got to stop the bleeding first," said Mrs Abbott. "Where's your first-aid box Mrs Pemberton?"

"We haven't got one; only things like sticking plaster and Dettol. Nothing large," Mum said and she sounded defensive.

I handed the stable bandage and a wad of lint over the loose box door. Mrs Abbot sighed. "I'll do my best with this then," she said.

No one knew what was the matter with Stardust. He wouldn't get up. There were branches in his box too and in the end we decided that one of them had hit him on the head.

Mr Abbott had found Dad's old chain saw and was mending it. The dogs were still missing. Scorpio, Prince, Lorraine, Solitaire and Jigsaw were unharmed and wanted breakfast. Sultan had a nasty cut above one eye which was shut.

Then James appeared and said, "I'm going to see if I can get anywhere. I want to see whether Virginia is still alive. I'll try to get a doctor and a vet. And I shall keep an eye out for the dogs. What are they called?"

And I thought, how typical of James not to

know their names! 'Rascal, Ruby and Ruffian," I said.

Mrs Abbott had stopped the bleeding. She patted Shamus while he stood pathetically holding up his injured leg which was now encased in a stable bandage. "That's the end of his show-ring career of course. Thank God he's insured," Mrs Abbott said washing her hands in the bucket of antiseptic. "We'll have to sell him; he'll be scarred for life. Will one of you check on Susan please?"

I ran indoors. Miss Steele was feeling Susan's pulse. "It's very slow. I nursed in the last war, so I do know what I'm talking about," she said. "We need a doctor dear, if you can get one, we really do."

"James is trying," I said rushing back to the stables.

The day seemed to have lasted for ever already, though really it had only just begun. Everything seemed very quiet suddenly because the wind had stopped blowing. Stardust was still lying down and, once again, Lisa feared internal injuries. Tracey was crying. Mrs Abbott was examining Sultan's eye, while I was counting the nine trees down in our main paddock, including my favourite oak, and then Justin appeared saying, "I've just heard on the news on Daddy's car radio, the hurricane has hit all of Southern England. There's no trains running and all the roads are blocked. The emergency services are working at full stretch. And three people have died."

"Thank you Justin," snapped Mrs Abbott. "But Shamus needs a blood transfusion. Any news of a vet?"

"James is still outside on his bike looking, but I think the road's blocked. I think all the roads are blocked. I suppose we could call in a helicopter," I suggested.

"But there's no telephone," replied Mrs Abbott. "Why aren't you doing something for God's sake, Harriet? Take Limpet some hay and water."

"But we can't get into the shelter."

"Use a ladder then, or haven't you got one? Oh God, you Pembertons, you don't seem prepared for anything – no first-aid equipment, no chain saw working, no generator to feed into the electricity system. How do you think we're going to manage tonight Harriet? Have you any candles? An oil lamp? Have you anything on hand for an emergency?" Mrs Abbott said accusingly before going into Stardust's loose box, her shoulders twitching with anger and frustration.

I shouted for Ben. "We need a ladder to feed Limpet," I said. "Because we can't get into the shelter without one, because of the fallen tree."

Then James returned saying, "The road's completely blocked by fallen trees. The electric and telephone wires are down all over the place. Nothing is working, absolutely nothing, and half the chimneys have gone off the almshouses."

"No vet, or doctor then?" I asked.

"No, not a hope."

"Did you see the dogs?"

"Not a sign."

Ben helped me put the ladder up against the shelter. He climbed up it and I gave him armsful of hay, which he dropped through the holes in the roof. Then we filled up a bucket with water and lowered it into the shelter the same way on the end of head collar ropes joined together. Lots of water slopped out, but there was a little left as it landed on the ground inside the shelter. And all the time Limpet watched us with startled eyes.

"The Abbotts are running the place," I said. "Listen, the chain saw's working. Dad couldn't have mended it in a month of Sundays."

"Mr Abbott trained as an electrician. He's furious that we haven't a generator. He's torn a few strips off Dad. I don't know how it will be tonight. He doesn't suffer fools gladly," said Ben.

"You think we're fools then?" I asked.

"No. But you must admit we are woefully unprepared."

Lisa was checking our ponies, running her hands down their legs watched by Tracey. Justin was helping his father. Dad was clearing up branches, putting them in a heap which grew larger every minute. Then Mum called, "Coffee time."

We went inside. Colonel Hunter was leaning against the Aga. "It's the only warm place in the house and I'm so cold," he explained. He looked very old. Suddenly he had become a tired old man. Miss Steele and Mrs Tomson were knitting with hot water bottles on their knees, bulging under blankets. Susan was sitting up and shouting over and over again, "Where's Jim. I want Jim."

"She's concussed, no one knows who Jim is. She may go on like that for hours. I think I'll go crazy soon," Mum said. "Mrs Abbott is dealing with everything outside. Our ponies seem okay," I told her. "But hers are banged about. Stardust won't get up."

"Perhaps he's concussed too," replied Mum with a wan smile.

"And we need a vet."

"Perhaps you could get help on a horse," she suggested.

"But if I got there, how would the vet or doctor get back?" I asked.

"I've tried biking. It isn't possible," said James entering the kitchen. "There are trees down on the road. Nine in a row and all enormous, I counted them, and even a horse couldn't get over them."

"Thank God for the Aga. At least I can prepare a meal," said Mum.

"Until the food runs out," I suggested.

"Yes, we'll be on tinned milk by tomorrow

morning," Mum said. "And there's no more bacon."

"Porridge. We'll live on porridge," said Colonel Hunter. "The Scots live on porridge, damned good stuff porridge."

Miss Steele was stroking Susan's forehead. "It's all right dear, Jim is quite safe. He will be here presently, not to worry dear," she said.

I drank my coffee. "I'll go and help with the mucking out now," I said.

Mrs Abbott inspected every loose box as I mucked it out, saying things like, "You've left some muck in the corner over there Harriet," and "I think you need a little more straw Harriet. It should be banked up round the sides of the box, that's better."

Ben was enjoying himself with a bonfire. Lisa and Tracey were on the common calling the dogs.

"If horses stay lying down for more than a few hours they die," said Ben presently looking over the loose box door, where I was cleaning around Stardust.

"I think Stardust has given up," I said.

"I think we should make him get up, that's what I think," argued Ben.

"Not without asking Mrs Abbott," I answered.

"The Abbotts are running the place," Ben said.

"There was a vacuum, no one filled it, so

they did," I said. "And anyway Stardust belongs to them."

I squatted on the straw and stroked Stardust's ears. They were hot, and there was sweat behind them, and on his neck.

"I think he's in pain. I think it's serious," I said slowly. Ben joined me inside. Together we felt him all over. There was nothing wrong with him as far as we could see, and yet he still lay there as though he was afraid to stand up, and the sweat behind his ears could only mean one thing – fever or pain.

"We ought to get him up," Ben said again.

"Not without Mrs Abbott," I insisted once more.

Then a small voice said, "He's mine. Get him up please."

I looked up at Tracey and Lisa who were leaning on the loose box door. Tracey was crying. Lisa had an arm around her shoulder. "We can't find the dogs anywhere," Lisa said.

Ben handed me a head collar. I slipped it over Stardust's neat, well bred ears. And now I was frightened of what might happen and of what we might see. I think we all were.

"He's such a lovely pony," Tracey said slowly. "He was going to Wembley next year. I was going to ride him there. He would have won, I know he would, and then I would have had another cup."

"Who cares about damned cups?" Ben snapped back.

"Mummy likes me to win cups," Tracey replied wiping her eyes.

"You can't go on doing things for Mummy all your life," said Ben.

"Shut up, she's only eight," I said.

I pulled gently on the headcollar rope. Then Mrs Abbott's shadow appeared across the doorway. "Who said you could get him up!" she said.

"I did Mummy."

"You don't heed an eight year old child, do you Harriet?"

"But if he stays down much longer, he'll die," Ben told her.

"You're right of course. Pull gently on the rope Harriet, gently. Give him time to think about it."

I was sweating now. Supposing he can't get up, supposing his legs are broken, supposing he needs putting down and we can't get a vet? I thought.

Stardust grunted. He strengthened out his forelegs. They looked normal, clean tendoned with neat fetlocks and lovely round hoofs. Yes, he would win at Wembley I thought, if he could walk, if he wasn't maimed in some hideous way for life. If he didn't have to be put down, as soon as a vet could be found.

"Pull gently Harriet."

"I am Mrs Abbott," I said.

"I don't think his hind legs are working properly," suggested Ben kneeling down to talk to Stardust, to say, "Poor old Stardust.

What is it then? What's the matter?" To find a few crumbs of oats in the pocket of his battered husky, to hold them out to Stardust, who wouldn't touch them, who hadn't touched any food all morning.

"Shall I pull a little harder, Mrs Abbott?" I asked.

She was in the box too now. "Yes." She wasn't crying. Perhaps if you've been a nurse you can stand more than other people, I don't know. But she was quite calm, she had been calm all morning. She had lost valuable dogs; Sultan was scarred for life and could at any moment start bleeding to death. Shamus' eye might never recover, and now Stardust didn't want to move his hind legs.

Mum would have been at breaking point. I felt like crying myself and he wasn't my pony. But Mrs Abbott remained dry-eyed, more like a general than anyone else I thought. A general who could have his troops massacred and get up next morning and eat a good breakfast.

"Get him up Harriet. Pull him up. I want to see what's the matter with him," cried Tracey suddenly.

"He'll die if he stays down much longer," Ben reminded me.

"Come on Stardust. Stand up, hup," I shouted while Ben pushed at his quarters and the others stood watching, as though we were the servants and they the bosses.

Stardust threw his head up. His front hoofs

clawed at the brick floor beneath the straw.
His eyes rolled, his hind legs strained and
then he was up, a trembling liver chestnut
pony, one hind leg out of line dragging
behind the other.

"He's broken his leg. Look Mummy, look."
shouted Tracey. "It's his off hind. What are
we going to do? Will he have to be put down
Mummy? Will he?" Then Tracey stared at
Ben. "Can you put a horse down?" she asked
in a shaky voice. "Because he's in agony, isn't
he?"

Ben shook his head. "It's out of the question. I'm not a vet," he said.

Then Mrs Abbott walked into the box.
"Whoa pet," she said. "Steady." She felt Stardust's injured hind leg with gentle hands,
talking to him all the time. "He's slipped his
stifle," she said finally. "We can't put it back
unfortunately. Get him a feed Lisa, just
damp bran and pony nuts. I'll go indoors and
get a sedative for him. I've got a syringe. I'm
always prepared for anything." And I knew
that it was true, which was doubtless why
the Abbotts were rich and we were poor; they
had proved to be superior by their actions
because none of us could have mended the
chain saw or stop a wound bleeding or inject
a sedative into a horse's neck more skilfully
than a vet as it turned out. "He'll be all right
now for a bit. Give him his feed Lisa," she
said a few minutes later.

Colonel Hunter was outside now dragging

bits of fallen tree about. He was wearing bedroom slippers and with his white hair standing up round his ancient face he looked very old and fragile. I could hear Dad saying, "Take it easy Colonel. You don't have to help. I'd stay in the warm if I were you."

"Must do my bit. I've always done my bit," Colonel Hunter muttered, his blue-veined hands dragging a branch towards a gigantic heap of them.

Shamus' wound had started bleeding again. The dogs were still lost and it was eleven o'clock now and there was still nothing moving outside the gates of Black Pony Inn, not a car nor a lorry, not the milk trolley nor the post van, and already I was longing for normality.

Six
No way round

Once again Mrs Abbott tried to stem the blood streaming down Shamus' leg using a clean sock this time to plug the hole which was there.

"He's worthless now. He'll never be sound again Harriet," she said sounding tearful. "Please try calling the dogs once more," she added.

Outside one could hear the distant whine of chain saws. Across the common people stood aimlessly at their gates. Outside Lilac cottage a car had been crushed by a fallen tree. There was no sign of anyone inside it.

I stood and called the dogs until I was hoarse. I asked people whether they had seen them. But they only shook their heads and a woman wearing a headscarf told me that Mr Brind's cows were down on the railway line, but the line was blocked so it didn't matter. An old man, who walked with the aid of a frame, said that he had never known anything like it. The new telephone box had blown over. An old dilapidated barn lay in pieces on the ground. Heaps of tiles lay beneath a bungalow's hanging gutters.

People were cutting up fallen trees. Bonfires sent grey smoke into the grey sky. The storm had changed everything. No one had gone to work. We were cut off. And some of the new houses near the church relied on electricity for everything! Somehow it made all my previous fuss over the Abbotts seem trivial. This was life, real life. All the rest was unimportant, I thought, going back to Black Pony Inn across the familiar common, where trees lay like fallen giants, trees I had known nearly all my life, trees which had stood there for centuries. Somehow it put everything in perspective, made Tracey's love of silver cups seem even more ridiculous, and my sadness over the loss of my bedroom futile and selfish. It made me understand why Colonel Hunter harped on about the last war; for ordinary life must appear rather trivial after you have faced death for so long and watched your friends die.

But now Lisa was calling my name. I started to run. "I'm on my way," I shouted. "What do you want? I can't find the dogs, I've looked and looked."

"Mum wants you and Ben to try and get a doctor. Colonel Hunter' had a stroke," she called. "Hurry. She won't let me go, but Ben is tacking up Solitaire and Prince. And Mrs Abbott wants a vet. Hurry up. Run. It's a major catastrophe."

I was breathless when I reached the yard. "We'll never make it," I gasped.

"We've got to try," Ben said.

"Is he very bad?"

"I don't know. He's not talking and his face is twisted. Mrs Abbott is dealing with him. He should be in hospital of course," Ben said matter of factly, though I sensed he was upset.

Lisa fetched my riding hat. Suddenly I didn't feel like talking.

"Dad and James are trying on foot. They've heading for the railway line," Ben said mounting Solitaire.

"It's blocked by fallen trees, everything's blocked," I answered glumly, mounting automatically, turning Prince round, riding out of the yard across the changed common, which was suddenly like a mouth with all its teeth gone. "The roads are blocked, we'll have to try the fields," I said.

"Miss Steele is crying. I think she's in love with Colonel Hunter," Ben said.

"And Susan?" I asked.

"She's still shouting for Jim."

"And Mum?"

"She's near breaking point."

"And the Abbotts?" I asked, dismounting to open a gate.

"He's trying to clear the road; she's exhausted. Tracey is screaming because she can't watch television, and Justin is waiting for the next new bulletin on the BMW's car radio," Ben said.

Our horses kept stopping suspecting an

enemy behind every fallen tree. Prince was on edge; he wouldn't walk and stared around him as though seeing everything for the first time. The air still smelt of burning wood. In the distance the railway line was empty of trains, and the roads were empty of cars. It felt eerie and frightening as we cantered across a ploughed field on our nervous horses, who were only waiting for a chance to carry us back to their friends at Black Pony Inn.

A tree lay across the gate out of the field. Ben looked over it. "We can jump the hedge further down, there's quite a good roadside verge," he said.

"And then?" I asked.

"God knows. It's in the lap of the gods. But we must remember that while we hesitate, Colonel Hunter may be dying and Shamus bleeding to death," replied Ben.

I imagined us attending Colonel Hunter's funeral. Or would some distant relative whom we had never seen and who had never bothered about him, appear to claim everything and have his remains removed to some distant crematorium? I wondered gloomily.

We collected our horses together and rode them at the hedge. There was a drop on the far side and we only just missed landing on the road.

"Hurrah, now we can go on," cried Ben pushing Solitaire into a trot.

"Funny, there are no cars on the road," I said.

"They're probably holed up in their garages," replied Ben optimistically. "It can't be more than two and a half miles to the Health Centre now."

"Let's hope there's doctors there waiting for their patients. But it doesn't seem very likely, does it?" I replied. "And what about the vet? He won't be in his surgery either."

"The town may be different and it's only two miles on along the main road now. And I'm sure that will be open. It must be," said Ben.

I thought that Ben would make a good officer in the army. He would lead from the front and never give up.

"I don't want Colonel Hunter to die," I shouted above the clatter of our horses' hoofs. "I should miss him too much."

"Miss Steele would miss him even more," replied Ben.

But now we saw that two enormous sycamore trees lay stretched across the road. Two men were looking at them.

"Can't we get through?" shouted Ben.

"What does it look like?" shouted one of the men.

"Haven't you got a chain saw?" asked Ben halting Solitaire.

"Ours isn't big enough. Besides they're too heavy to move. It's a job for the council, if they ever get round to it," the other shouted.

"We need a doctor. It's urgent," I said.

"I'm sorry to hear it, but we all need something we can't get."

"Are the telephones working around here?" asked Ben.

"No way. I should have been on the six-thirty a.m. train to London for a conference," said one of the men. "And here I am. And I can't even inform them that I won't be there. It's a joke."

After a moment the other man said, "It's a rum old job isn't it?" He looked as though he had lived in the country all his life and had never been to London or the sea.

"Isn't there a way round?" asked Ben.

"No, there's no way round, not until the council have cleared the trees."

"A man's had a stroke and we need a doctor," insisted Ben.

But they were tired of us and turned away and trudged towards cottages further down the road.

"We'll have to go back," I said to Ben.

"And admit defeat," Ben replied, making defeat sound like a dirty word.

"At least we tried," I answered.

"There must be a way," insisted Ben, but he didn't sound convinced any more.

"If only the telephones worked," I said.

"What difference would that make; they still couldn't get to us," retorted Ben.

"Yes they could – by helicopter," I cried and imagined Colonel Hunter being taken inside a helicopter on a stretcher.

"It'll be dark soon," said Ben pushing Solitaire into a trot.

It took us ages to get home. We were both filled with a sense of failure and our horses stopped at every fallen tree again. The Solitaire refused three times before he would jump the hedge.

"There's no decent run, that's why," explained Ben when at last he was over and we were crossing the plough again.

"Mrs Abbott will call us feeble," I said as we rode across the common.

"She can try herself then," replied Ben.

When we reached home, we turned our horses out and watched them roll. Everything was quiet in the stable yard. Without electricity, we'll have to feed early and go to bed early. What a bore, I thought.

"There are fallen trees all along the railway line. And no one's clearing them," said James appearing as we removed our boots. "So it's going to be a long while before we can go anywhere."

"You're preaching to the converted. In other words, we know," Ben snapped back.

Mum appeared next calling hopefully, "Any luck? Did you find a doctor?"

I shook my head while Ben said, "We did try Mum."

Someone had brought a bed downstairs for Colonel Hunter. He was sitting up on it, looking incredibly old. His face was still twisted

74

but he could talk out of the corner of his mouth, though not very clearly.

"He mustn't get excited," Lisa told us. "He'll be all right if he doesn't have another stroke. He's very lucky." I had the feeling that Lisa was quoting Mrs Abbott.

Mum had kept us some lunch. "You really couldn't get through then?" she asked.

"Not a hope in hell," replied Ben.

"After you've eaten your lunch, I want you to light fires in the old ladies' bedrooms; otherwise they'll die of cold. There's plenty of wood now. If they have fires, they'll have a bit of light too. They won't be so nervous then," Mum said.

"But the fires haven't been lit for years. What about the chimneys? Shouldn't they be swept?" asked Ben, who Mum often says has an old head on young shoulders.

"Never mind the chimneys. Just try," she answered. "Please . . .'

So after lunch we gathered sticks and wood and prepared to light the fires. First of all we had to sweep up the mess which had fallen down in the chimneys during the hurricane. Then Ben laid the fires carefully criss-crossing the sticks in the small Victorian grates. Mum had told us not to use many matches. "I've only got three boxes left," she had said. "So don't waste them please."

While Ben worked, I fetched more logs and put them in old coal scuttles, which had not been used for years. Then Miss Steele appeared and started to advise us in her plaintive voice, which James had once, unkindly, likened to a cat mewing. "You must have air underneath the kindling," she said. "Here, let me show you."

"But look it's going!" cried Ben triumphantly. "And the one next door is going too, so now it's up to you and Mrs Tomson to keep them alight. Mum says I'm to put some of the Aga fuel on later, then they'll stay in all night. But we must see to the horses now, because it's getting dark outside," finished Ben.

"What about the Colonel?" asked Miss Steele anxiously.

"He's going to have a bed in the kitchen. And Mum has found a nightlight she bought for Lisa when she was ill years ago, and never used, so he'll be all right. And anyway I think Mum and Dad are going to sit up with him all night, poor things," Ben said.

"I don't mind doing a shift," said Miss Steele.

"Lovely," said Ben. "You're an angel Miss Steele," and with that we escaped out to the stables and more problems.

The chain saw had broken again, so no one had released Limpet from the shelter where he now stood anxious, hungry and neglected. Mrs Abbott had revived after two hours in bed and was doing what Mum calls laying down the law again. Partly recovered, Susan

76

was going through her things in the caravan assisted by Lisa. They were both crying. Tracey was feebly brushing Stardust. Justin was sitting in his father's car, once again listening to the radio. (He had done little else since the hurricane.) Mr Abbott had disappeared. Mum said that he was looking for a pub where he could buy some whisky. James was trying to reach Virginia. And above us all, the grey sky was darkening into another night.

Mrs Abbott stared at me angrily. "Your mother says she only has a few candles left Harriet. How are we going to manage? I cannot understand it, I really can't. A house full of old people and no emergency form of heating; it's incredible," she said. She looked changed. Her hair had lost its bounce, her eyes were no longer enhanced by eye shadow, so that now she looked wan and rather ordinary, and not at all rich. Suddenly I wasn't scared of her any more.

"We only have three old people with us, as you know, we have a further four beds for guests, and we're all quite young," I answered. "So the house is hardly full of old people."

"Well have it your own way, Harriet, but I still think it's incredible," she said.

"But we've never had a hurricane before," I answered.

She made no reply, and now the wind had started blowing again and it frightened me,

77

for the roofless loose boxes were a constant reminder of what it could do. Then Justin appeared. "They've brought in men from all over Britain, even from Northern Ireland, to re-connect the electricity," he said. "But there's more gales on the way."

"What about the telephones and the roads?" I asked.

"The authorities are doing their best." Justin was beginning to talk like the radio news.

"Aren't you going to help with the mucking out?" I asked.

He shook his head. "I never help. It's Susan's job," he replied.

"But Susan's hurt," I answered.

"She can do them tomorrow then," I looked at his small set face and I thought, he's ruthless. He's a hard-headed company director already. Perhaps people are born suitable for certain jobs. Perhaps we're already programmed before we ever enter the world.

Meanwhile Lisa and Ben fed and watered Limpet and the horses in the fields. It was nearly dark now and Stardust still didn't want to move so I took his food to him – just damp bran and nuts and an armful of hay. I took his water to him too, holding the bucket under his nose while he drank.

"The vet will put his stifle back, but it may not stay back," said Mrs Abbott watching me. "I think we're going to have to start all over again."

"What do you mean by that?" I asked anxiously.

"Put them all down, and buy another lot."

"But they're not washing machines, they're alive, friends," I cried.

"Oh Harriet, one has to be realistic, however much it hurts," she said.

"But can't his stifle be strapped up?" I asked.

"Have you ever tried bandaging a stifle Harriet?"

I shook my head.

"You can't," she said.

"Plaster then . . ." I suggested, but she only smiled grimly.

And now it was dark. Justin drove his father's BMW into the yard and switched on its lights.

"No more than five minutes Justin dear," Mrs Abbott told him. "Because we don't want a flat battery, that would be the last straw."

In the lights from the headlamps I swept up the yard and topped up the water buckets in the loose boxes. None of the Abbott horses had been out and their legs were beginning to swell. They were all on bran mashes and Mrs Abbott had started to demand carrots. But now, as we walked indoors together, there seemed to be a strange sort of friendship growing up between us; we were opposite in nearly everything, but somehow we were meeting halfway. I suppose one could call it an unexpected affinity growing between us. Mrs Abbott had opened a new window on life for me and I was beginning to see it from a different angle. I was beginning to see us from the outside, from someone else's point of view for the first time. And it wasn't comforting.

"I've seen Virginia and she's all right," James was beaming as we returned indoors. "I even got as far as the village shop, but it has no candles left, or milk, or matches."

Tracey had found one of my old pony books and was reading it. Dad and Mr Abbott were lighting a fire in the open fireplace in the hall, which we had never used before. Ben stood nearby with a pair of ancient bellows in his hands. We are going back in time, I thought, back to the 1800s. Colonel Hunter was talking incoherently to Miss Steele. Mrs Tomson was talking to Justin about the early days of radio. Lisa was outside calling the dogs again. She seemed to be forever calling them and her voice was growing hoarse.

I helped Mum serve tea. Then we drew all the curtains and lit our few candles and I think we both were praying that the lights would come on soon, before the candles were burnt out.

The fire cast shadows across the hall. It lit up the paintings there. It was an evening I would never forget. If we had been on our own, I might even have been happy. But with our demanding guests this was impossible.

"I can't see to read," shouted Tracey.

I fetched a torch and gave it to her.

Mr Abbott paced up and down the hall. "Are you sure we can't get to a pub?" he asked presently.

"We can try again," Dad replied.

"I feel so dirty. Is the bath water hot? And is there any light up there?" Mrs Abbott asked.

"No, sorry, the immersion heater isn't on and the Aga doesn't run to baths," Mum said.

And Mrs Abbott sighed and her sigh said many things.

Then Mrs Tomson and Miss Steele started to play cards by the light of a candle while Ben sat twiddling his thumbs. Then Lisa came indoors saying, "I can't find the dogs. "I've looked and looked, and now there's a wind blowing and it's pitch dark. What are we going to do?"

"Nothing," said Mrs Abbott, which surprised us all, because she had never said anything like that before.

James sat silent thinking, I suspect, about Virginia.

"We'll eat early tonight. It'll only be soup, I'm afraid," Mum said apologetically, stirring the contents of a saucepan by the light of a candle.

"But I never eat soup," cried Tracey.

"You can eat bread and cheese then," Mum snapped back.

Mrs Abbott was sitting with her head in her hands now. I felt sorry for her

"At least we are still alive and so are the horses," I said.

"But not the dogs. We've lost the dogs," she replied.

"They may turn up. We mustn't lose hope," I answered.

"I expect someone's shut them in a barn," suggested Ben.

"And while there's life there's hope," added Lisa.

And it seemed strange that we were comforting Mrs Abbott.

We ate our soup out of bowls in semi darkness. We left the washing up until morning. Ben and I had a torch between us. There was no moon. It was one of the blackest night's I've ever known. And the wind was starting to howl again like some poor demented animal trying to get inside the house.

"They won't be able to mend the electricity tonight," Ben said, climbing into bed, before handing me the torch.

"I always thought the old days must have been lovely with horses everywhere, now I'm not so sure," I said. "I can't see how they managed without electricity."

"What you've never had you don't miss," Ben said.

The torch was flickering now. In another minute it would need a new battery and we had no batteries in reserve and no means of getting any. I could hear Dad and Mr Abbott arguing downstairs. Dad was shouting,

"You'll get a reduction in charges, of course you will, so what are you griping about? I'm sorry about the drink. We just don't keep a lot. We don't have a licence."

I pulled my duvet over my head and prayed. God make them mend the electricity soon. God bring back the Abbott's dogs and make Stardust sound again. But I knew God wouldn't listen to me, because I never went to church. So why should He?

Seven
"We'll be ruined"

I hardly slept that night. The wind shook the window panes and howled. My room had grown cold during the day and was even colder in the night. And I was dreading the next day. I imagined the last candle burnt, stocks of food growing low. And now we had Susan to feed as well. What if we ran out of everything? I had seen inside the bread bin; we were down to two large loaves, and we had no yeast to make fresh bread, no strong flour, no more candles, no more meat, and only powdered milk. We wouldn't have minded. But the Abbotts would. They would go on and on about it. And Colonel Hunter might grow worse, he might need invalid food, steamed fish, tapioca pudding, that sort of thing.

Next door Ben was moving about in his bed too. And twice Lisa called the Abbotts' dogs' names in her sleep. And now I couldn't help worrying about them, for Ruffian was barely recovered from his accident. How was he managing? Would we ever see any of them again? And now it seemed unlikely, for they could be so easily captured and sold for four figures.

At last morning came with rain driving across the fields in sheets, driving water under the back door, soaking everything outside. I sat up in bed and thought of our horses out in it. I imagined Limpet trapped in the shelter with the rain pouring in. I dressed and went downstairs, and in a sudden burst of hope, tried the telephone, hoping against all reason that it had been repaired, so that we could call assistance − vet, doctor, food van. But of course it was still dead. Everything seemed dead at the moment. The milk had not been delivered. The postman was nowhere to be seen. I went outside. Our horses were standing together in a corner of the bottom field, their backs to the rain, their tails tucked between their hind legs, their heads low, their ears back. There was nothing to recommend the day, absolutely nothing. I looked over the loose box doors. Stardust was lying down again, the others were resting various legs. Only Scorpio's head was restlessly hanging over his door.

I went outside, through the archway onto the common. Nothing had changed there, the trees still lay where they had fallen, the road was still empty of traffic. The rain stung my face. My eyes ran, my hands turned to ice. At that moment there seemed no reason why the weather should ever change. I dragged hay into the bottom field, while Limpet whinnied pathetically from the shelter. My boots squelched in mud, the rain ran off my husky onto my trousers and into my boots. My hair dripped rain down my neck, and there was no crack in the grey sky, no hopeful sunlight, just the pouring rain, as endless as an ocean. I swore then that, when life was normal, I would never grumble again. I would never be nostalgic about the past, or long for the days when all the houses were old, and the motor car had not been invented. I will thank God for the telephone and electric power every day, if only it will return I thought, before I heard Mum calling, "Harriet where are you? Come in out of the rain. Come in at once."

"In a moment. When I've fed Limpet," I shouted back.

I fetched hay and climbed the ladder which still leaned against the shelter, and my feet kept slipping on the wooden rungs. Limpet raised his head and whinnied. He was soaking wet and shivering. I pushed the hay through the cracks in the broken roof and my coat sleeve caught on a piece of wood, and suddenly the ladder was gone and I was falling down and down into the wet earth.

I lay under the ladder. Dimly I heard Mum calling again, "Harriet where are you? Come in at once."

She sounded miles away. I felt dizzy. I felt sick. I couldn't move without wanting to vomit. And still the rain poured down.

Quite soon after that I realised Ben was bending over me. "Oh Harriet. Why didn't you wait? Why are you such a fool?" he asked.

"Actually I'm quite all right," I replied carefully, trying to sound normal though there was a buzzing in my head.

"I'll get help," Ben said and disappeared.

Presently Dad carried me indoors. "Another casualty," he said, putting me down on a chair in the sitting room.

"Poor Limpet, he's shivering," I told them.

"Shivering's a good thing, it's nature's way of keeping something alive," replied Mrs Abbott briskly. "It's when a horse is cold and doesn't shiver you are in trouble."

I lay looking at the dust which was gathering everywhere. And when Dad helped me out of my wet coat, bits of hay fell onto the chair and carpet, and now there was no cleaner to pick them up because it too needed electricity.

"How are you feeling?" asked Mum handing me a mug of tea.

"All right. I can't think why I'm being so feeble. I think it must be shock. One minute I was feeding Limpet, the next I was on the ground," I answered. 'It all happened so quickly."

"Don't ever go up that ladder again, unless there's someone on the bottom rung," Mum said.

"We must get Limpet out. Surely we can cut the tree up bit by bit,' I suggested.

"My chain saw can't handle a trunk that size," Dad replied.

"We'll have to take the shelter to bits then, plank by plank, because he can't stay there another night," I said.

"Let's wait until the rain stops," suggested Mum.

Colonel Hunter was shuffling about in slippers now. Susan was recovered and wondering about her boy friend who lived in Kent.

I ate cereals for breakfast with powered milk. Ben was relighting the fires in the fireplaces upstairs now. James was bringing in logs, dripping rain onto the hall carpet.

"They'll never burn. They are too wet," he said.

Tracey was still in bed reading. Justin was still sleeping, cosy under Ben's duvet. Mr Abbott was pacing the hall fuming.

"This is absolutely typical of this country. One small hurricane and everything packs up. Listen, there's isn't even a train running. It's pathetic."

"Perhaps one should unwind occasionally," Mum suggested.

"Unwind! We're all too laid back already," Mr Abbott stormed. "That's what's wrong with this country."

The rain beat against the window panes. Our horses were still out in it. Limpet was still trapped in the shelter. Some days seem endless. This was one of them. We seemed suspended in time. The sense of frustration was enormous and everywhere. I saw Mr Abbott kicking at the wellington boots lying in the back porch in rage and frustration.

James tried the telephone again and then hurled a mug across the kitchen, which smashed against a wall. Ben was biting his nails to pieces. Mum's face was drawn with worry.

Later as the rain slowed down, I went out to clean the stables with Susan and Mrs Abbott. Lisa had gone upstairs to play monopoly with Justin and Tracey. Ben found a hammer and started dismantling the shelter.

The horses were a little better. Stardust stood up with difficulty. Shamus' wound had stopped bleeding. Sultan's injured eye was half open. "You see we've managed. Nothing's died. Perhaps doctors and vets are not so important after all," said Mrs Abbott.

"We couldn't have managed so far without you," I said, and meant it.

"But I haven't done much, not anything really," she replied.

"But you were here when we needed you. You knew that Colonel Hunter and Susan weren't going to die. You knew what was wrong with Stardust. The rest of us thought his leg was broken. Without you we would be crazy with worry," I cried.

"Thank you Harriet. That's the nicest

thing anyone has said about me for years," Mrs Abbott replied, and kissed me.

I was so surprised that I nearly dropped the fork I was using.

"And you're all right Harriet. You'll go a long way one day. I know that. Just a little more dedication. And you're going to be beautiful, a really beautiful girl."

"Me beautiful? That's a joke," I answered, but was pleased all the same.

"I mean it. I always mean what I say."

"Thank you."

The sky had cleared. A watery sun looked down on us. Everything began to seem a little better. Ben led Limpet out of the shelter. "I'm going to give him a warm feed. I think he deserves it," he shouted.

"He's a good boy. I hope Justin grows up as good," said Mrs Abbott her eyes following Ben across the yard.

"But Justin is so dedicated and so clever," I answered. "He can even programme a computer already! It's fantastic."

"Yes, that's true," said Mrs Abbott with a sigh.

Then James appeared shouting. "There's a helicopter landed, there are men mending the wires. Come and look. We're going to have electricity again."

The helicopter was parked on the common. There were half a dozen men. Two of them were already reconnecting cables.

"When will the electricity come on again?" called James.

"Not yet. Not for some time. There's over fifty poles down," one of them called back.

"It's a beginning anyway," said Mrs Abbott.

There were baked potatoes for lunch topped with cheese. Mr Abbott left half his. Colonel Hunter still couldn't talk properly. The chain saw had broken down again. It was very cold in the dining room where the guests ate. Susan joined us in the kitchen saying, "I'm not one of them. Never have been. Never will be."

Tracey demanded ketchup. Justin demanded pickle. Mr Abbott seemed to be sitting surrounded by a magnetic field of anger. When we left them alone to eat their pudding of stewed apple I could hear him shouting at Mrs Abbott. "You chose this place. You wanted to move. It's all your fault."

Tracey was crying. Justin said, "Leave Mummy alone, Daddy. You wanted to move too. You wanted somewhere smart to entertain your business associates. Remember?"

The Abbotts had seemed so perfect. Now I realised that they were just as flawed as the rest of us, and I didn't envy them any more, not their horses, nor their equipment, nor their clothes, nor their individual television sets; not even Justin his computer. I was happy to remain careless, clumsy, untidy Harriet Pemberton without a penny to her name. I didn't even want their swimming pool, and with this feeling came a great sensation of happiness for I realised that the saying, "money doesn't buy happiness," is probably true.

"They're cracking up," I said.

"They can't be," replied Ben without asking who "they" were.

"Mr Abbott is used to things running his way. He wants to push on and he can't," suggested Mum.

Later when it was dark, we played games by the light of the open fire in the hall. Then we told stories. Justin's was about a world ruled by computers. Lisa's was about a pony which no one could ride but a girl, who turned out later to be a ghost. Ben wouldn't tell a story but James' was called "Murder At Black Pony Inn", and went on and on growing more and more spooky so that when it finally ended no one wanted to go to bed.

"Why don't you tell nice stories," Mum wanted to know.

Finally I went to bed without a light, feeling my way upstairs, undressing in the dark. I didn't wash or clean my teeth, just crawled under my duvet and waited for daylight to reappear, my mind thinking back over the last two days, thinking of all the things we might have done but hadn't.

Next morning nothing seemed changed. Except that life seemed to be moving at a slower pace; only Mr Abbott was functioning at the same speed as before. Susan and Mrs Abbott rode out on Sultan and Scorpio, who after too much time cooped up were full of bucks. Ben and I carted logs upstairs and into the house where we stacked them by the Aga, while Mum removed the last piece of meat from the freezer.

Stardust wasn't any better. Shamus' injured leg was enormous. Suddenly there seemed no end to our worries. Miss Steele would no longer go up or down stairs in the dark. "I can't risk a fall," she said. "I'll have to have a chamberpot in my room, what my mother called 'an article' ". And we hadn't a chamberpot for we had never imagined such a catastrophy. At eleven o'clock I found Mum sitting alone in the kitchen, her head in her hands.

"There's going to be an accident," she said looking at me with a tear-stained face. "I know there is. And then we'll be sued. And the insurance will wriggle out of it, they always do, and we'll be ruined. I can see it happening Harriet. Miss Steele will fall downstairs or Colonel Hunter will fall out of bed, or Tracey will trip over something and hit your bed with her face and break all her front teeth. I can see it clearly Harriet. And there's no more food in the deep-freeze, and no way of getting any. And it's all my fault. I should have forseen this situation. I should have had a generator installed. The Abbotts are right. We've failed everybody."

It was a terrible moment. I didn't know what to say. I'm not used to grown ups crying.

"It could go on for another week, do you realise that Harriet? Then the old people here will die of hypothermia. One by one in their freezing bedrooms," Mum continued in the same hopeless voice.

"But they have got fires," I said, putting my arm around her shoulders. "So they'll be all right. Don't worry."

"Yes, thank God for grates and fireplaces, and the Aga. Without them we would be finished. At least we can cook, and there are still a few potatoes left in the sack in the pantry. What about the horses?"

"We've got plenty of hay, but everything else is running a bit low. Luckily since most of them are standing idle they don't need a lot of oats," I replied.

I suppose in every catastrophe there's a low point, when hope is abandoned and all seems dark and hopeless. And this was it. The Abbotts refused to drink powdered milk in their coffee or tea. Colonel Hunter was very cold. Mum plied him with hot-water bottles and hot drinks, but nothing seemed to help. Looking at him made me afraid he might die at any time, and what would we do then? Once again it would be Mrs Abbott who would decide. But she seemed changed too; there were new lines etched on her face. She talked about the dogs in the past tense.

"We had hoped Rascal would win at Crufts in February," she said. And I imagined other cups, even bigger ones this time. She talked of having Stardust put down. "He's finished," she said. And none of us could bear to look at Shamus' leg any more because it was enormous now and he held it up all the time looking at us pathetically, as though saying, "Do something – please". "He needs a shot of penicillin and I haven't got any," Mrs Abbott said. Justin wearily told her that everything was going to be all right and she snapped back, "Don't be a fool, Justin, and don't treat me like one either."

Mr Abbott was at a loose end. He constantly disappeared in search of something – a mended telephone? a cleared road? No one was certain. "I'm losing thousands every minute, do you realise that?" he shouted at lunch time banging the table with his fist. "And what's this?" he continued, staring at the almost meatless hotpot which Mum had prepared. "Is this all the grub we've got left?" And no one answered him.

Miss Steele refused any lunch and sat feeding Colonel Hunter mashed potatoes with a spoon. Mrs Tomson kept on about rationing in a war no one besides herself, Miss Steele and Colonel Hunter remembered. Dad went without lunch too, saying, "Leave the food for the guests. I need to lose some weight."

Susan sat getting in everyone's way and grumbling. She had managed to salvage two bags of crisps and a tin of baked beans from the caravan. Now she ate them like a hungry dog.

"Why didn't they tell us it was going to happen?" asked Ben presently. "I mean, why do we have weather bulletins if they can't get it right? I mean what's the point of them Mum?"

"They do their best. The wind must have changed at the last minute," replied Mum, who seemed prepared to forgive anyone everything at the moment, if only they would forgive her for her lack of foresight.

Then, after lunch, I started to feel sick. It wasn't a usual sort of sickness. It was to do with fear. I was sick because I was afraid that we were going to be cut off for weeks, that our old guests would die, and the Abbotts go crazy with frustration. Odd though it may seem, I was not afraid for us. We seemed to have an enduring strength, which the Abbotts with their drive and boundless energy didn't possess. For they were tiring themselves, and burning up everything they ate, with anger and frustration. Even Justin seemed to be losing his nerve, for without electricity he had no computer to play with and no television to watch. And Lisa was cracking up too. Now that Limpet was all right, she worried endlessly about the dogs. Every hour she seemed to be on the common calling their names, on and on, and there still wasn't a sign of them anywhere.

We went to bed early that night for without lights there was no point in staying up. Dad still had a torch working, which he used every hour to look at Colonel Hunter asleep in the hall now beside the big, still smouldering fire. Dad too was afraid that he might die, just slip away in the night leaving us to deal with his remains as best we could.

Later that night I heard Mr Abbott shouting. "It's a disaster, an absolute disaster. If this goes on another week we'll have lost everything." Mrs Abbott was crying.

I was glad now that we hadn't any money to worry about and that Dad wasn't raving like a lunatic over his assets. I was glad I didn't go to St Peter's too, where I suspected houses and money were a major part of conversation. After a time I found myself praying again. "God, please bring back the dogs and save Shamus, Stardust and Colonel Hunter." And I was ashamed because without thinking I had put Colonel Hunter last. Then Lisa appeared like a ghost and, drawing back the curtains, said, "Look there's a moon outside. What's going to happen Harriet? I'm so frightened. Will Shamus and Stardust really be shot?"

And I didn't know what to say because I didn't know either. "Things happen; it's fate," I said at last.

"Tracey's been crying all evening. Mr

Abbott is being horrible. Justin won't speak to anyone, not even to me, and I haven't done anything to him," Lisa said wearily. "When do you think the lights will come on again?"

"Soon, very soon," I said without conviction.

Lisa curled up at the bottom of my bed. "I suppose wars are like this," she said.

"Worse, much worse," I answered.

"I wish I could find the dogs. I really liked them," she said presently.

"One day we'll be able to laugh about this," I answered. 'I'll say, do you remember the hurricane . . . ?"

"When Colonel Hunter died, and the dogs died, and Stardust and Shamus were shot. Oh yes, what lovely memories!" cried Lisa sitting up again. "Oh Harriet, you're just as mad as everybody else."

"Well why talk to me then?" I asked.

"I won't," she said, and went back to her own room in a huff.

And when sleep came at last to me, it was like a friend shutting out the fears and anxieties which were everywhere.

Eight
My heart sings

I had baked apple for breakfast next morning. The Abbotts hadn't appeared by eight o'clock, only Mum was in the kitchen making tea. I went outside and found Susan mucking out.

"God, I'm sick of this. I feel as though I'm in a cage," she said.

"But why?"

"I can't ring up my mother. I can't ring up my boy friend. And there's no post, that's why," she shouted, pushing the wheelbarrow with such force that it keeled over.

"We can still ride," I said.

"Ride, ride, that's all I ever do."

"Lucky you."

Shamus' leg was so big now, it made me sick to look at it.

"He's getting blood poisoning, that's what he's getting. Look at the lump under his elbow, go on look," thundered Susan.

"I don't want to," I replied.

"And Stardust's finished too. And no one's doing anything. It's so damned pathetic. Surely someone could walk to the vet and bring him here," Susan continued furiously.

"Why don't you go," I answered.

"I am. This morning. You can come with me, we'll take bikes," Susan said.

"Okay. Great. As soon as I've finished feeding," I said.

So half an hour later, we pumped up the tyres on James' and my old bike and set off. And, as we pedalled, miraculously the roads seemed to be clearing in front of our eyes. Men were everywhere with huge machines and gigantic trucks. They waved cheerfully as we passed. And the bikes didn't shy or buck or stop at every fallen tree, and so suddenly we were on the main road, pedalling like mad. "It's open and we never knew," I shouted.

"Oh God, I feel so free," shouted Susan laughing. "I feel as though I've been let out of prison. I feel terrific."

"And so happy," I yelled back.

Now I liked Susan, but at that moment I was in the mood to like anybody, such was my feeling of relief. Suddenly the main road and the cars passing along it were beautiful. Everything was beautiful. We reached the suburbs. Lights were on; everything was working.

"We've wasted so much time," I shouted pedalling faster and faster. "And won't the Abbotts be furious? There they are, lying in bed, not knowing that that road's open."

"Oh the Abbotts!" shouted Susan. "It's

money, money, money with the Abbotts. And win, win, win."

I could see the vet's surgery now. Another minute and we were throwing down our bikes and rushing inside. "It's urgent. We need Roy," I cried to the receptionist.

We always have Roy to tend our sick and injured animals. He's a friend as well as a vet.

A minute later he was standing in front of us saying, "Hallo Harriet, what's up?"

And I was so excited that I could only gabble, "We need you straight away, we've been cut off. We've got blood poisoning and a slipped stifle, the lot."

"Can you come at once?" Susan added smiling.

"Will do. Give me twenty minutes. I must finish surgery first," he said, the same bluff, down to earth Roy we love.

We leapt on our bikes again and pedalled another hundred yards to the human Health Centre. The receptionist wanted us to sit down, but we refused and soon we were seeing a new, young doctor with lovely dark wavy hair and blue eyes. I explained the situation. ". . . so one stroke and a lot of pending nervous breakdowns," I finished.

"Including me. We've been cut off for days and it seems like years," said Susan smiling into his eyes. "We're all going mad."

But he didn't smile. I suppose that doctors

don't find madness funny, and I don't blame them, because the real thing must be awful.

"I'll be there as soon as I can," he promised, while the receptionist, who wore a white coat and plastic framed glasses, wrote down our address saying, "Are you sure the road's open? Doctor's very busy this morning and we mustn't waste his time."

"Of course it's open. How do you think we got here?" replied Susan. "We haven't got wings, we can't fly unfortunately."

I wished she wouldn't be so rude, because we will have to talk to the receptionist long after she's gone.

We went outside together. "Stupid old cow," said Susan mounting her bike.

We pedalled full speed home, standing on our pedals, hoping to race Roy there, laughing and screaming at one another, like two horses turned out after being shut in for weeks on end.

"I'm so happy," shrieked Susan.

"Same here," I cried.

"And wow, what a doctor, you are lucky," shouted Susan her fair hair streaming behind her.

"I'll hit you with something, then we'll call him out," I shouted back.

"Oh yeah. I bet he wouldn't come. I bet they would send some old boy who's been a doctor for years," laughed Susan.

All the fallen trees had gone from the road. All the telegraph poles were up again. The sky was blue. Birds were singing. People were starting up cars, clearing up their gardens, laughing. A milkman was delivering milk. The red post van was rushing from house to house. I felt as though I had been away for a long time and come back. Tears of joy ran down my face as I pedalled. My heart sang.

"I'm moving back into my caravan tonight," said Susan. "I'm tired of sleeping on your sofa. And I'm going to ring up Jim. Your Mum won't mind will she?"

"Not if you put some money in the box and time it," I said.

We could see Black Pony Inn now. Wood smoke was rising from the high tudor chimneys.

James was waiting by the back gate. "How dare you take my bike without asking?" he shouted.

"You were in bed. You weren't up," I shouted back.

Susan was laughing. I started to laugh too.

"We're saved. The road's open. Is the telephone working yet?" I asked.

"No. And Mum needs the doctor. Colonel Hunter's had a relapse," James said.

"Well he's on his way. So's Roy. The emergency is over. Everything's going to be all right from now on. Isn't it fantastic?" I shouted.

"You had better tell crosspatch Abbott that; he doesn't know yet. He's fuming over breakfast, because there isn't any milk, or bacon and eggs, or sausages. He's being absolutely foul," James said.

"But listen, there's the milk trolley. Can you hear it?" I yelled in triumph before I rushed indoors shouting, "Everything's all right, the road's open. The doctor's on his way, and the vet. We're saved."

Mum stood in front of me with tears of relief streaming from her face. Mr Abbott leapt to his feet shouting, "For goodness sake why didn't you tell me before, Harriet? Look at the time I've wasted."

"Because I've been visiting the doctor and the vet. That's why. How's Colonel Hunter?" I cried.

"Very poorly," Mum said.

"I'll go into town right away and find a telephone," cried Mr Abbott leaving the house at the double.

"I'll go and get some food for us all," Dad said hugging me.

"I can't believe it. But it's too late isn't it? The dogs have gone. And Shamus is going to die of blood poisoning. Oh God, I can't bear it," cried Mrs Abbott with her head in her hands. "I can't bear another minute of it."

"But it's over," I cried.

"Not just that – the move, the work, the bills," she cried.

Luckily there was a knock at the door then and we found Roy outside. I introduced him to Mrs Abbott and we hurried to the stables

104

together, Mrs Abbott wiping her eyes and saying, "I'm sorry I'm such a wreck." (As though Roy was looking at her or cared!) Then Mum opened the back door to call, "The electricity's on again. I can't believe it, everything's working."

Roy talked quietly to Shamus, while the big horse smelt him. "Poor old fellow, what a shame," Roy said slowly, squatting in the straw and feeling his leg. Then he went outside to his car. "Antibiotics?" asked Mrs Abbott.

"Yes, and a pain killer, for starters," Roy said.

And Lisa appeared from nowhere to ask as usual, "Is he going to die?"

"Not if I can help it," replied Roy filling a syringe. "But he isn't well, not by a long chalk."

No one else can give an injection like Roy; he just slips the needle under a horse's skin so gently that the horse hardly feels it. "Okay, we'll have the bandage off. He needs walking out. He shouldn't be standing still," Roy said. He looked at the wound. "I've got a new type of dressing I'll put on, it's part seaweed and very good," he said returning to his car.

Tracey had joined us now. "Justin's gone into town with Daddy," she said.

"Right," said Roy now. "Lead him out in an hour's time, just gently. He'll be a bit sleepy, but not to worry because if he's too energetic he'll start the bleeding again. Now let's see the other patients." Stardust looked a pitiful sight, almost a case for the RSPCA. His sides were run up like a greyhound's, his eyes were dull, his head hung low.

"More sedative," said Roy with a sigh going to his car. "I don't know whether I can get his stifle back in place; otherwise he'll have to go to the Equine Centre at Newmarket for an operation."

While Roy waited for the sedative to work we showed him the other horses. "You've done quite well considering," he said. "At the stud they've lost one of their best mares. A tree fell through the roof of her box. And she was in foal too. The foal would have been worth thousands."

"Is Stardust going to be all right? That's what I want to know," cried Tracey staring up at Roy, her eyes full of tears.

"I'm going to do my damnedest to save him. But no promises," Roy replied.

"To save him?" cried Tracey.

"Well he can't live in pain, can he?" Roy said. "He can't be left as he is either, I must do something or he'll have to have an operation. There's no other way. And even the operation may not work; nothing is one hundred per cent in my trade. We just do the best we can."

Mrs Abbott watched Roy with glassy eyes. She was so tired that I don't think she was really with us. Something had happened in the night. Something between her and Mr Abbott – that was obvious. But no one knew what.

. "Oh Harriet," she said now. "The horses pull at your heart strings, don't they? Mine too. Will you keep Stardust for us, for ever?"

"Not if he's in pain," I answered wiping a tear from my eye.

"I don't think I can bear to have him put down. I shall go away for a day and leave it to you," she continued. And now I seemed to be seeing the real Mrs Abbott for the first time, the mask had gone. (Perhaps we all wear masks at times.)

"Ben's stronger emotionally than I am. I'm not being sexist, but he's the person to deal with such things," I answered, but even as I spoke I wasn't sure that this was true, because Ben *will* deal with anything; but afterwards his hands come up in a rash, or he has to reach for his asthma spray. Then I thought that the results of the hurricane would be with us forever; so that any future wind would revive memories and fears.

Later Roy drank a cup of tea in the kitchen. The young doctor had arrived and was arranging for Colonel Hunter to be taken to hospital by ambulance, which made me think that if only he hadn't assisted in helping us, he would be all right now. Miss Steele stood in the drive watching him leave. Colonel Hunter waved weakly to us all calling in a voice crackling with age, "It's only for assessment. Keep my room, will you?"

"Of course. It'll always be ready for you," Mum called back wiping tears from her eyes.

Then Susan asked the young doctor to look at her head. "I'm sure it should have been stitched. The caravan fell on top of me. It was horrific," she told him smiling.

I went back to the horses with Roy, and I kept thinking that if the Abbotts hadn't been with us, our horses would have been trapped in the loose boxes instead of theirs, so that in a way we were lucky. Ben joined us and led Shamus out of his box, gently, talking to him all the time. He was very stiff, but gradually as he walked up and down the drive slowly, he improved, until after some five minutes he was almost sound again.

"He's going to be all right," said Roy smiling at Mrs Abbott.

"But not for showing," she answered.

"No, he'll have a scar of course."

I couldn't bear to watch Roy working on Stardust's stifle. But Ben did. Outside the back door Susan was saying goodbye to the doctor. Tracey was playing some sort of ball game with Lisa. The sun was actually shining, and the clouds in the sky were small and cheerfully buzzing about like strange ships in a blue sea.

"I've won," shouted Lisa.

"No you haven't, I have," shrieked Tracey.

Then Mum appeared to say, "The dogs are

found. They're all right. They're in a dogs' home. They were found nearly ten miles away searching for food on a garbage heap."

"Excellent, we'll fetch them after lunch, shall we?" Mrs Abbott cried smiling at me.

"If you want to, that's all right by me," I replied.

"There's a special lunch – roast beef, roast potatoes and all the trimmings, to make up for the last few days," Mum said before going back to the house.

"I've put his stifle back, but I don't know whether it will stay. I've strapped it up the best I can. I'll be back tomorrow," said Roy, whose car telephone was calling him urgently to another job.

Susan appeared then asking for instructions. I went indoors to lay lunch. It seemed to have been a very long morning.

"We're out of the wood," said Mum happily.

"I seem to be fetching the dogs after lunch. Mrs Abbott seems anxious that I should go with her. I can't think why," I said.

"She likes you, that's why," Mum replied.

"Oh yeah," I said.

Everyone, except poor Colonel Hunter was present for lunch. Dad opened two bottles of wine. "It's on the house," he explained. "A sort of celebration. After all several people have died, but we are still here, in spite of everything."

"Just," said Mrs Abbott. "But I can't drink because I'm driving."

"I suppose we have to go back to school tomorrow?" asked Justin.

"It's been lovely and awful at the same time," said Tracey smiling at me as I poured wine into glasses. "And I don't want to go back to school. I wish I could go with Lisa to her school. It sounds much more fun."

"Don't be silly Tracey," snapped Mr Abbott scowling at her.

"She may have a point," said Mrs Abbott.

"What point? You can't compare the two schools, they turn out different people," replied Mr Abbott.

"What rubbish Dad," cried Justin.

I returned to the kitchen unable to believe my ears. Was it really the Abbotts talking – Justin? Mrs Abbott? Had we changed them after all? Then I heard Mr Abbott say, "I've seen the solicitor. Completion is next Tuesday. So we'll be leaving then, lock, stock and barrel."

"On Tuesday? As soon as that?" asked Mrs Abbott. "But supposing we can't move the horses?"

"They'll have to follow later then."

"I don't want to go," cried Tracey. "I want to stay here with Lisa and Harriet. I like it here. I want to stay here for ever. I don't like the new house, it's too big and empty and I don't want a swimming pool, or a jacuzzi. I want to stay here Mum. Are you listening? I like it here."

There was a short silence. We could hear

everything from the kitchen. Ben looked at me and said, "What a turnabout!"

"She's a spoilt brat. I wouldn't say no to a swimming pool," said James. "And think of the jacuzzi! Wow!"

Then we heard Mrs Tomson say quietly, "Money isn't everything."

"But it makes a hell of a lot of difference," answered Mr Abbott.

"Perhaps we could leave Tracey behind," suggested Justin with a snigger.

Mum started rattling the dishes then. "Stop eavesdropping," she said. "It's a disgusting habit."

"We're not eavesdropping. We just can't help hearing," I answered.

"And I feel like crowing," added Ben smiling.

"I don't want Tracey and Susan to go, especially Susan," said Lisa. "I want them all to stay here for ever, and the dogs."

"Where will our ponies live then in the winter?" I asked.

"We can build some more loose boxes," Lisa said.

"No thank you. I want a rest. I've had enough of the Abbotts," Mum told us dishing up trifle. "Mr Abbott is a pain, and I don't suppose Peggy will return, she hates them too much. She says they treat her like dirt."

"I don't hate them any more. I'm sorry for them. I'm just glad Dad isn't like Mr Abbott.

I would hate having to win all the time," I said.

"He beat Justin for not winning last year. Tracey told me," Lisa revealed. "And Justin didn't shed a tear."

"I don't believe you," I said.

"It's true. He beat him in the horsebox. Ask Susan," Lisa answered.

And now suddenly I was seeing Justin differently too. I couldn't imagine dear good-natured Dad beating anyone or anything. He simply isn't made that way. But what if he had beaten us? We would be different then. Meaner for a start, crueller too, withdrawn. Like Justin? I didn't know for sure. We're not perfect, far from it, but supposing Dad had beat us? It was too awful to contemplate. And supposing he beat Mrs Abbott too?

"It's only gossip," Mum was saying. "You mustn't listen to gossip."

"I don't think Lisa gossips. I think it fits," said Ben slowly. "Poor Justin. And I've been hating him. I've refused to talk to him, and I've refused to bowl for him or put up stumps. I feel guilty now, because he probably needs someone to talk to."

"And Tracey hates St Peter's. She wants to go to school with me. She says she's going to run away," Lisa continued and now she sounded important, because we were all concerned and listening, and we rarely listen to Lisa, because we think of her as the youngest in the family, a sort of perpetual toddler.

112

"They're leaving soon. We may never see them again," said Ben.

"I know. And we've hated them, most of the time anyway," I replied.

"And envied them their money," Ben added.

"You don't have to feel guilty. Lots of fathers beat their children. Justin will surely repeat the pattern and beat his," replied Mum sadly. "That's the way it goes."

"It doesn't have to," said James.

Our guests were filing out of the dining room now. I missed Colonel Hunter, who would always look into the kitchen before going into the sitting room for coffee. He would smile at Mum and say, "That was very nice Mrs Pemberton. Thank you."

Miss Steele and Mrs Tomson were talking to each other. The Abbotts were now silent. Soon they'll be gone, I thought, and I didn't know whether to be pleased or sorry.

Nine
Time to leave

We checked the horses again before we set off to bring home the dogs. Lisa and Tracey squeezed into the back of Mrs Abbott's car. I sat in the front. Everything was normal again, or almost, and it was like a miracle. The only black spots were the trees still lying everywhere, the houses with gaping holes in their roofs, the fallen fences and smashed sheds.

"It was the worst hurricane ever in this part of the world," Mrs Abbott said, driving at high speed. "We're lucky to be back to normal. In parts of Kent, they're still without electricity."

"We'll be better prepared next time. Dad's talking about getting a generator. We were to have a swimming pool, but he thinks the generator will be more use to the guests," I said.

"He's probably right. I can't see your present guests using an outdoor swimming pool," said Mrs Abbott, while Lisa and Tracey giggled in the back. (As thick as thieves, Mum would have called them.)

There were dogs everywhere at the

kennels. Lost dogs, dogs no one wanted, dogs which had never known a home. Bitches in whelp. Puppies and high spirited dogs. Misunderstood dogs. They were in pens watching us, some begging to be taken away, others looking for beloved owners, only to be disappointed. They were all shapes and sizes, some pedigree some not.

"Where do they all come from?" cried Lisa in despair.

"From all over the place. We have most soon after Christmas. They are given as pets then, and are soon found to be too much trouble," said the large lady who was showing us round.

"And if no one ever claims or wants them?" asked Lisa, her voice shaking with emotion.

"We find them homes."

"And if you can't?"

"If they're old or vicious, or diseased, we put them down." The woman who was called Mrs Chivers seemed very matter of fact. I suppose she had to be, for to be involved emotionally would break one's heart.

The Abbotts dogs were all together. They welcomed Mrs Abbott with wagging tails, while I stood staring at a black and white dog whose nose was pressed tight against the bars of his pen, who had eyes as soft as velvet, with so much sadness in them that to look at them was to weep.

"Hasn't he got a home?" I asked.

"Apparently no one wants him. He's been

here a month and no one's taken him," said Mrs Chivers. "Why, do you like him dear?"

"Yes I do." The dog was wagging his tail now, slowly, uncertainly, his eyes on my face.

"We need a dog," I said. "We really do."

"But you haven't asked our parents," cried Lisa.

"He's half labrador, half collie. He's a real sweetie and very clever," said Mrs Chivers.

Lisa was looking at him too now. She had always wanted a dog, more than me. At times it had seemed an obsession.

"We can ring up Mum," I said. "Have you got a telephone?" And all the time my heart was racing inside me with hope, and I was seeing the dog in the kitchen lying by the Aga. And watching me leave on the school bus in the morning, and still there when I returned in the evening.

"It will be a very good home. I can vouch for that," said Mrs Abbott. "I can give you a written reference if you like."

In the end we went indoors and rang up home. Mum wasn't certain at first and kept saying, "You must ask Dad first."

"But we need a guard," I replied. "And he's quite big, but not too big, big enough to frighten people anyway; and he's got a lovely face. Please Mum. Please."

Then Lisa grabbed the telephone and cried, "You promised we could have a dog, you know you did, and Dad did. Please Mum."

I knew it wasn't true. No one had

promised, but Lisa's not above inventing things which have never happened, when it suits her that is.

When at last it had been agreed and we had put down the telephone Mrs Chivers said, "I shall have to ask you for a donation. We always do." And I hadn't any money with me, nor had Lisa.

"That's all right. He's going to be my present to you both. I owe you a lot and I was going to buy you something," said Mrs Abbott briskly, taking a cheque-book out of her bag. "Shall we say fifty and something for my dogs' keep?" she asked writing the date on a cheque.

"We'll pay you back," I said. "Truly."

"Yes, truly," agreed Lisa jumping up and down with joy.

"I just hope we can fit them all in the car," replied Mrs Abbott signing her name. "Four of us and four dogs, it's quite a lot."

We wrote down our names and addresses, and Mrs Abbott signed a form.

He answers to 'Bob'," said Mrs Chivers. "He belonged to an old man who died. He's six years old." She put a lead on him. "You can keep it if you like," she said.

I helped Mrs Abbott with her dogs. They were very excitable, pulling and choking in their haste to get into the car. Fortunately it was a very large car.

Bob sat on the floor in the front with me,

while the other dogs sat in the back part, panting.

"I don't know what to say. You've been fantastic Mrs Abbott. Thank you so much . . ." I began wishing to be polite.

"Don't say anything then," replied Mrs Abbott driving onto the road. "The best things are left unsaid."

Bob pressed his nose against my knee; then he put his paws on my lap and tried to lick my face. I can't believe he's ours, I thought. We've wanted a dog for so long. And now, thanks to the Abbotts, we've got one. The Abbotts of all people!

"A penny for your thoughts Harriet," said Mrs Abbott.

"Nothing fantastic. I was just thinking how much we had all changed. Somehow the hurricane changed everything, not just the landscape but us too," I said slowly, hoping she wouldn't laugh at me as James would have done.

"Yes, you're right. It blunted the sharp edges, put things in perspective. All that need to win seems pretty silly when things are crashing all about you, and the food's running out," replied Mrs Abbott turning to smile at me. "We were all pretty uptight, weren't we? You didn't like giving up your room; and I don't blame you. We didn't think the arrangements were good enough," she continued.

"How did you know about my room?" I asked turning red.

"It was on your face, all the time. And you didn't like giving up the stables either."

"I didn't know it was so obvious," I said.

"It doesn't matter. It's over now. Let's just be friends. God knows we all need friends. And remember this, Harriet, if any of you ever need help with schooling your horses, I'm around. We're only going to be twenty miles away and that's nothing in a motor car. So just ring me up day or night," she finished.

Bob settled in very quickly. Everyone loved him. The Abbotts began packing. School started again. Shamus' bandage was taken off for good. Stardust was turned out in our smallest paddock for a few hours every day. His stifle was still in place and he was no longer in pain. "I won't call again unless you call me. I think we've won," Roy told us as he left for the third time.

The first frost came and the last of the flowers in the garden wilted away. The new loose boxes were mended. But nothing could replace the trees. It would take a hundred years to do that. And without them we could see things from our windows which we couldn't see before – the church, the road, even sometimes the railway line. Bob seemed to like us all equally and our elderly guests loved him. Mum visited Colonel Hunter in hospital with Miss Steele. They took him flowers and chocolates and orange squash.

"We should have taken him whisky," Mum said afterwards. "But we were not sure whether it was allowed."

Mrs Abbott gave me a last lesson on Prince. Ben put up a small course of jumps and before I jumped them I trotted over poles on the ground trying to get him to relax. I had learned more than I can possibly describe with Mrs Abbott. Prince had been hollowing his back and rushing his fences; now at last he was taking them steadily, his back rounded.

"You've got a winner there," Mrs Abbott told me when the lesson was over. "He's clever, he's fast and he's careful. You don't often get those three altogether in one horse."

As we walked indoors that day, I told her his history. How he had come to us as unrideable, and then refused to live anywhere else. How he had appeared in a film with me when we swam a river together.

"So he isn't really yours at all?" she asked when I had finished.

"Not completely. He really belongs to the film company," I said. "If they want him for a part we have to let him go."

We went out to dinner with the Abbotts that last evening. Mr Abbott paid for everything. I had nothing suitable to wear. In the end I wore one of Mum's dresses which was corduroy and blue. She lent me a necklace to go with it. Justin stared at me all through dinner. I didn't know what to say for no one had ever looked at me like that before. Tracey and Lisa giggled together and pretended to be drunk. Ben talked to Mr Abbott about his future. James wasn't there, preferring to spend the evening with Virginia. We drank to all sorts of things, to eternal friendship, to the end of the catastrophe, to the Abbotts's new home, to our future.

We felt sad and merry at the same time. It was a fantastic evening when no one said a cross word. Afterwards Ben, Justin and I sat talking in the playroom. Cider had loosened Justin's tongue. Words poured out of him. He asked me to go to the Christmas disco at his school. I didn't know what to say. I thought of telling my form at school about it.

They wouldn't believe me at first. "You go to a disco, Harriet? At St Peter's?" they would cry in disbelief. "You? How will you bear to leave your horses?"

Because of that I said "yes", for I was tired of being considered old-fashioned, and I knew I would enjoy their envy. At the same time I was worrying about what I would wear.

"You don't have to bother too much about clothes," Justin said, reading my thoughts. "Jeans will do."

Then he told us about his parents, how his Dad had started as a labourer, then became an electrician, how hard it had been until he had invented a new sort of foam for cushions and upholstery which wasn't inflammable. He had invented a lamp too which was shaped like a lozenge. He had borrowed money and gone into business and made a fortune. "But he's always wished he was educated, that's why we're at St Peter's. Justin finished. "He wants us to have what he didn't have. He wants us to have an easier time than he did. People laughed at him you see, or so he says. They laughed at his clothes, at the way he spoke."

"You wouldn't think it now," Ben answered.

"No, he even has his hair set. It's that important to him. if I told the chaps at school that, they would laugh their heads off," Justin said.

When we said goodnight to one another it was lovely to be able to switch the lights on in the attic, and wash, and go to bed and read. To know that tomorrow the lights would still be working, that the fear and the discomfort were over. Already Mum was looking years younger, while Dad was praying for a cold snap so that people would start wanting double glazing. It seemed years since the Abbotts had arrived, though it was really only a few weeks. Their visit had caused a watershed in our lives Dad was to say later.

I couldn't sleep that night. It was a very

still night, without a whisper of wind, silent too. Not the rustle of a bird or the squeak of a mouse, with the branches on the trees quite still at last.

When we returned from school the next day Mrs Abbott and Susan were loading their horses. Lisa was watching them with tears streaming down her face.

"For goodness sakes," I cried seizing her by the shoulder.

"I don't want them to go," she sobbed. "Not any of them."

"You'll start me off in a minute," I said wiping my eyes.

Their horses loaded one by one without a backward glance, while ours watched, their eyes glowing with interest.

Mum and Dad appeared to shake hands with the Abbotts one by one, saying things like, "All the best," and "You know we're here if you need us."

Justin and Tracey stood saying nothing.

The cars were loaded with computers and suitcases. The dogs were leashed and ready to leave. Bob stood with us watching. Susan had cleaned out the loose boxes. Everything was tidy. It was like an end of an era.

"Right," said Mrs Abbott at last. "Time to leave. Come on kids." Justin shook hands with Ben. Then he kissed me.

"See you," he said and walked away without looking back and I swear he was crying.

Mrs Abbott kissed us one by one. "You

know the door is always open. Come whenever you like. Here is our change of address card," she said, her voice shaking with emotion.

There was nothing left to do now but wave and wave until they were out of sight.

"I hate farewells," Mum said then. "Come indoors. There's a surprise."

"What surprise? I don't want a surprise. I want them back again," cried Lisa tearfully.

We found presents for each of us on the hall table – a picture for Ben, a book on riding for me, a china horse for Lisa, and an address book for James. Then Mum said, "Follow me." And there in the old pantry was a generator. "So we're all right now whatever happens," Mum said happily.

"But they gave us Bob," I cried. "We didn't need other presents. We didn't need other presents. We didn't need anything."

"They've left one for Peggy too," Mum said. "And for Colonel Hunter. They've been very generous."

"So in spite of the catastrophe they *did* like it here," said Lisa sniffing.

When we returned outside, our horses were standing waiting by the field gate, and I knew they were asking, "Can we go into our loose boxes now?"

We fetched feeds and put them in their mangers. Then we opened the gate, and with one accord they hurried each to his own box and own manger.

"They're pleased anyway," said Ben shutting the gate after them. "Now I'm going to move back into my own bedroom. I feel just like they do. As Colonel Hunter would say, enough is enough."

"Same here," I said.

My room had been left tidy and propped against the mirror was a note which read: *Thank you for letting me have your room Harriet, it's the nicest in the hol world*, Luv Tracey XXXXXXXXXXXX

Bob followed me upstairs. I sat on my bed and he put his head on my knee and licked my hand. I sat remembering the emotions and trials of the last few weeks. I remembered how I had hated the Abbotts and how the hurricane had made us friends, changing us all. And I thought, perhaps we need disaster to make us see life as it really is. To get rid of jealousy and envy and offence and all the other awful things which beset us.

Then Mum called "Tea. There's lardy-cake."

And drying my eyes, I thundered downstairs with Bob at my heels.

"We have a new guest arriving next week. He's a young army officer on leave. He's called Captain Matthews. His favourite aunt lives nearby and he wants to ride," Mum told us cheerfully.

And helping myself to lardy-cake, I thought, here we go again.

While Ben said, "He can ride Solitaire if

he likes, because I haven't much time this term."

"I want to visit the Abbotts, Mum," Lisa said. "Soon."

"We'll all go," said Ben. "We can swim in their pool, because I know we'll never have one whatever Dad says."

And now the future stretched ahead full of hope. Christmas, a disco, the beginning of another year – they lay before me like a landscape waiting to be explored. "I don't know why, but I feel as though I've grown older," I said taking a piece of lardy-cake.

"About time too," replied Ben laughing.